Murder

in

Parts

by
Amber LaCorte

Krackle
Publishing
USA

Murder

in

Parts

Editor
Larry Krackle

ISBN: 978-1984169570

Chapter 1

What they were about to do was taboo, even in their world. Around one PM they met at Denny's to talk about it over lunch. After eating, she hopped into his car.

He gave her a long, tender kiss. She brushed her impeccably-styled blonde hair back with a hand and responded by wrapping her arms gently around his neck.

"Are you sure you want to do this?" he asked.

"Yes, I'm sure. I've thought about it long enough. I love you."

He drove the three blocks to a Super 8 motel. She anxiously waited in the car while he went into the office to pay for a room.

When he returned, he turned to her. "This is your last chance to back out."

She gently placed a hand on his cheek and replied, "I'm ready to do this."

They had been seeing each other for several months. It hadn't taken her long to fall in love with him.

The slender man with thinning brown hair exited the car and walked around to the passenger side. Opening her door, they walked hand in hand to the room he rented. Once inside, he gave her an eager kiss as he slowly backed her toward the bed. Reaching the bed, he started undressing her, one piece at a time. He removed her blouse first. The he kissed her passionately, first on the lips, then down her throat and finally onto breasts being held in by a bra he desperately wanted to remove. Slowly he slipped down each strap. Then he reached around and attempted to unfasten the clasp. It defied his attempts.

What a dodo, can't even undo a bra. Guess I'm too excited.

She put her hand on his arm. "Wait." Reaching behind her, she unfastened it herself.

Next he reached down to undo the fastener on her jeans. Unable to unhook it, she grasped it instead and opened it. She unzipped her jeans and slid them down her legs. She sat down to take her shoes and socks off. Then she stood up. He pulled her panties down.

Standing naked, she unbuttoned his shirt and he slid his arms out of it. While he held his arms to his side, she unfastened his jeans. They dropped to the floor. Last, she pulled his shorts down.

He laid the woman he really did love gently onto the bed. Then he climbed on top where he performed the most passionate lovemaking he'd ever experienced.

The dark clothed figure watching the motel room from his car just experienced a terrible gut wrenching scene he hoped he wouldn't see. He just saw his wife go into a motel room with someone he thought was a friend. He followed her because he wondered if she was really going where she *said* she was going.

A countless number of thoughts raced through his mind. *How could she do this to me? I thought we were happy. What have I done or not done that made her want someone else?*

Then he thought about his friend. Instant fierce rage overtook him. His heart felt like it was going to leap out of his chest. *You son of a bitch. You're going to pay for this.*

He settled back into his seat and waited for them to come out of the motel room.

It was about an hour later when the passionate lover looked at the time. Kissing her gently, he said, "I think we better go. They'll start wondering where we are."

"I almost don't care if they find out about us."

"Me too, but right now, we don't quite know what to

do about my wife and your husband. Next time, we need to talk about that. I know I love you. I just don't know how and when to tell them."

He reluctantly left the bed and dressed, then gave her an emotional kiss. He didn't want to leave. He held her for a long time before he said, "Okay, we have to go."

They stepped out into the warm night.

He had become impatient. He knew what was going on in that room. Several times he nearly stomped to the door and pounded on it. It was hard waiting for them to come out of their tryst nest.

The door finally opened. They came out hand in hand. He kissed her as he helped her into the car. Extreme anger overcame him. It was inconceivable to him that she had been unfaithful to him. He thought he had a happy marriage.

Obviously he didn't.

Was it his fault? Was it her fault? He really didn't know. He only knew he didn't want to lose her, but what could he do about it? He watched the car pull out of the parking lot.

That's when he started formulating a plan to remedy the situation.

Chapter 2

An old hound dog crossed the street behind Safeway and headed straight for the dented dumpster. He sniffed the rusty corner, checking out markings from a Chihuahua, a Beagle and a Great Dane. Determined to reclaim his territory, he lifted his leg high into the air, attempting to match the topmost mark.

A cracked flowerpot fell from the sky, nailing him on the tailbone. It broke into pieces as it hit the ground. He jerked, yowled, then made a beeline for the dense wooded area across the alley, leaving a long wet streak behind him.

An elderly woman's head popped up from inside the dumpster.

"Huh? Who's dere?"

Her wrinkled hand grasped the edge of the dumpster. While she looked around, she scratched her dirty powdery-grey hair held in place by a rainbow knitted beanie. Satisfied the coast was clear, she resumed rummaging around, searching for her evening meal.

"I sure hope dere's gonna be somethin in here fer dinner. I'm hungry"

Maggie McGraw happened to be one of the homeless people in residence in the woods behind Safeway. Despite the police attempting to keep them out, they kept coming back. Hunger supercedes the law.

Her blue eyes, not showing the sparkle of her younger years, looked over the contents of the dumpster. She kept exploring the huge container, avoiding obvious garbage. She had become accustomed to the nasty smells she encountered. Dumpsters, as a rule, contained something that could be used for a meal. Maggie tossed aside a broken hanger, torn book and an old alarm clock.

"Hmm. Wait a minute."

Then she picked up the alarm clock again. Further inspection confirmed it truly appeared to be junk. She pitched it back into the dumpster. Sifting through more of the contents, something of interest caught her eye.

"Aha!"

Half a can of vegetable soup stood straight up as if it waited for her to find it. She placed it with care in the supermarket cart she took everywhere.

"That's today's lunch, but I still gotta have somethin fer dinner."

She dug deeper into the unpleasant receptacle and pushed a stack of old magazines aside. That's when she caught sight of a large package wrapped in butcher paper.

Maggie snatched it up. She pressed her fingers all over the outside of the package. A mental image of a roast came to mind.

"I hope it's not spoilt. I ain't had a good meal in a real long time."

Excited, she ripped tape off the package. When it opened, blood oozed from one end. She became more optimistic that it contained a sizeable piece of meat. A major portion of the contents lay exposed when she took off the last piece of tape. She took a good look at it. It appeared to be a hand, severed at the wrist, not a roast.

Maggie screamed and almost fell from the side of the dumpster as she jerked away. She threw the package back into the dumpster.

A sudden panic overcame her. She ran around the corner to the Safeway store. When she entered, she noticed a Starbucks in the corner. Still trembling from the horror in the dumpster, she hurried over to the blonde haired barista at the counter. Tears streaming down her face, she begged.

"Please, can ya call the cops fer me? I think dere's part of someone's body in the dumpster. I don't got a cell phone. Please?"

The shocked barista gasped. "Oh my God! Have a seat. I'll get you some help." She fumbled for the phone. Another barista fell into a chair to keep from fainting.

"Daniel, you gotta come quick. A lady just found part of a body in the dumpster."

The manager came barreling out of his office.

He took one look at Maggie. She definitely seemed extremely upset about something.

"Are you okay ma'am?"

Sobbing broke her speech as she said, "No! Dere's part of a body in the dumpster. It's a hand."

"Oh shit," he muttered quietly since he didn't want the disturbed woman to hear him.

"I'll call the police." He gave instructions to the baristas and rushed back to his office. "This is all I need. Who the hell would have done something so gruesome?" He dialed his cell phone and made the call.

While they waited for the police to arrive, the manager attempted to calm the old woman.

"That must have been a frightening experience."

Maggie clasped her hands to each side of her face and replied, "It was horrible."

The barista leaned intently over the edge of the counter to listen to the conversation.

Daniel said to her, "Give this lady a cup of coffee. I think she is in desperate need of one right now."

"Thank ya so much. It's bin a long time since I've had a fresh cup a coffee."

The manager took stock of the woman in front of him. Her face, devoid of makeup, revealed pale, furrowed skin, complete with crow's feet. Faded, stained, dark blue pants exhibited several patched holes and one large hole, not yet mended. She wore brown work shoes that looked too loose.

He decided it might help relax her if he could get her to talk about herself. "Tell me a little about yourself. Have you lived here long?"

Maggie stopped crying and wiped her eyes with a tissue Daniel gave her.

"When my husband passed away, I shared an apartment with my daughter here in Jamesburg. I was left without any income, so I di'nt have anywhere else ta go. Then my daughter died from cancer. I wasn't able ta get a job 'cause of my age. Too young fer Social Security and no money, I was without a place ta live agin. I chose ta be homeless."

It took a cop a few minutes to calm Maggie down enough to obtain the details of finding the shocking bloody package.

"Can you show me what you found?"

Maggie led them to where she threw the package back into the dumpster. She freaked out as they looked at the package. She started crying again.

One of the officers said quietly to another, "What kind of monster would do this, Bert?"

Bert replied, "I can't imagine even thinking about doing this to another person."

He turned to Maggie, "Do you live around here?"

"No, I'm homeless. That's why I was goin' through the dumpster. I was hungry."

"You staying in these woods?"

"Yes, I don't have any other place ta go."

Bert shook his head. "Okay, don't go anywhere till we check you out."

The police cordoned off the area with yellow crime scene tape. When they checked Maggie for warrants, they found none. The officers decided she wasn't guilty of killing and chopping up the victim since she indeed appeared to be homeless. However, they held her for the detectives to interview when they arrived on the scene.

Chapter 3

Detective Lee Cumming's cell phone rang. "Yes, Erica."

"Got a new assignment for you."

"Oh, great. Can't a guy take a coffee break? Cat and I are at Starbucks."

"Sorry Lee, but you need to kick it in the butt. This one's bad. Some lady found a body part in a dumpster."

"Oh, shit. Okay, we're on the way."

When the call ended, he turned to Catherine, his partner, "We gotta go, Cat. Someone found a body part in a dumpster."

"That must have been a shock. Just another day at the office for you and me."

"Yup, criminals never rest. That's why we will always have a job."

Catherine took the last swig of her coffee. "Okay, let's go find out who killed who."

While driving to the crime scene, she discussed what they might find. "It takes an obviously disturbed person to cut a body up," she said, her long, light brown hair falling softly around her face. It made her look younger than forty eight.

"Yeah," Lee replied, "another one of the sickos springing up everywhere in the world lately." He saw it several times during the four years he worked for the Detroit police department. When he moved to Jamesburg, Washington he joined the homicide squad and became a partner to Catherine Hendrix (also known as Cat). It gave the Jamesburg police chief someone with plenty of experience. Lee and Catherine solved several murders during the three years they worked together.

"Hopefully we can nab the jerk before he does it to

someone else." Cat remarked.

"I hope so too," Lee added. He glanced at the attractive woman sitting next to him. He never saw her without makeup. A hint of color enhanced her unblemished skin. Her eyebrows tweezed to perfection and filled in with color, looked like a work of art. Sensual red lips completed what Lee considered to be a flawless makeup.

Cat looked out the window. She enjoyed working with Lee. Although the shortest man on the Jamesburg police department, well developed muscles made him appear husky. He may have looked assailable, but she remembered numerous felons finding out different. She regarded his blue eyes as two dazzling pools of sky blue water.

Looking at him, she asked, "Did they say if it is a man or woman's body part?" She really didn't care. She wanted a reason to watch him.

"No, she didn't say."

Lee already lost a good portion of the hair on top of his head at fifty two. However, she viewed him as still being handsome.

He caught her staring at him. She quickly turned to look out the window again. Cat recalled when they first met. She worked on the homicide squad of the Jamesburg police department for five years. The partner she worked with for two years retired. That's when Lee was assigned to work with her.

Close to their destination, Lee caught her attention and said, "We're almost there." However, he went back to the things he liked about Cat. He suspected there was an unspoken attraction between them. He hoped it would become more than that. She had a body most women longed for. Men turned and admired her as they passed.

Perps soon found Catherine's beautiful body deceptive. She took numerous defense classes and surprised them when she took them down.

When Cat and Lee arrived at the crime scene, their thoughts and feelings took a back seat. They saw the police questioning a small crowd of people behind Safeway.

One of the officers asked a bystander, "Did you see or hear anything unusual?"

A slender man in his thirties replied, "No, I didn't see or hear anything. I'm here because I saw the cop cars. I just wanted to see what was going on."

When the officer finished talking to the man, he turned to the detectives. "Hi Lee. Hi Cat," he said, recognizing them from previous murder cases.

"Hey Todd, what've you got for us?" Lee asked.

"It looks like a man's hand. The homeless lady that found it is inside the Safeway store at Starbucks."

Lee laughed, "We just came from a Starbucks. We should have waited a few more minutes and had our coffee here."

Cat said, "Show us what she found in the dumpster."

Todd took them to the dumpster and handed them the package.

"Jesus," Lee said, shaking his head. "Okay Todd, before Cat and I talk to the lady that found the hand, we need to see if we can find the rest of the body. Assign one of them," he said, pointing to the other cops, "to go through the dumpster to see if there are any more packages in it. While he is doing that, we'll speak to the homeless woman who discovered the package."

Todd delegated one of the officers to the yucky task of rummaging through the unpleasant smelling dumpster. Then he escorted Lee and Cat inside Safeway to where Maggie sat at the Starbucks.

"Maggie, these are the two detectives who are going to ask you about what you found in the dumpster."

Cat began the interview. "Hi Maggie, I'm Cat and

this is Lee. Did you see anyone before or after you found the package in the dumpster?"

Still visibly upset, Maggie replied, "No, I din't see nobody. I just wanna get outa here."

"If you took anything from the dumpster, we need to have it back because it is part of a murder investigation."

"Only thing I took was half a can of soup. It's in my grocery cart."

Maggie took them outside and showed them the can of soup. It still stood upright in her cart. Catherine carefully removed it to preserve any fingerprints that might be on it.

They spoke to Maggie for a while longer. Then, since she seemed like nothing but a harmless old woman, they released her and watched her disappear into the woods with her cart.

The detectives returned to the dumpster to check on the progress of the cop going through it. When they reached the dumpster, Dr. Edward Danielson, the Medical Examiner arrived. Catherine and Lee became good friends with the Medical Examiner while working on some of their murder cases. Everyone knew about his reputation as a wisecracking M.E. He chose to be that way. He needed to keep his frame of mind light with a little humor to prevent his profession from getting too serious for him.

A smile lit up the face of the short, stocky man. "Well, what do ya know, I think I've met you guys before." He appeared to be in the same nonchalant mood as ever.

Lee replied, "I think we recollect you too.

Edward scratched the bald area on top of his head running between a substantial amount of hair. "I understand you guys got a little of some*body* in a dumpster." Then he waited for a reply.

"Oh, funny Ed. Keep practicing," Lee said with a

little snort.

They showed Edward the package with the partial remains of the hapless victim. During their conversation, he tested some more of his humor on the two detectives.

"Hey, have you guys heard of furniture disease?"

"Don't think I have. What is it?" Lee asked.

"It's when your chest falls into your drawers."

Both Cat and Lee laughed.

"Only you could come up with something like that Ed," said Catherine.

When the police finished fingerprinting the wrapping containing the hand of the victim, the M.E. opened it. He gave it a visual examination, then announced to Todd, standing next to him, "Yup, he's dead!" They both chuckled.

The cop assigned to search for the rest of the body, approached Cat and Lee. "I'm finished going through the dumpster."

Cat asked, "Did you find any other parts of our unfortunate victim?"

"No, I went through every inch, but didn't find anything else."

Lee turned to Edward and said, "I guess this is all there is for now. This is sure the strangest murder case we've ever had."

"I hope you find the rest of the victim."

Catherine said, "We have to check out all the dumpsters in the area."

"Well, I hope you find him before you check every dumpster in the whole city. That's a lot of dumpsters."

"I hope so too," Lee said as he shrugged.

Edward's cell phone rang. When he hung up, he said, "sorry, there is another case that needs me. I don't know why I'm so popular. I'll let you know what I find as soon as I finish examining what little bit is here. Bye Lee. Bye Cat. I would say it was nice seeing you, but under the circumstances, I don't think that would be the truth."

Lee said to Cat, "Even though everyone knows he's very thorough, his humor is sometimes a little gross."

"Yeah, but without it, he'd just be a dull Medical Examiner."

Edward laughed and as he left, he held up the package containing the hand. "I just hope I *don't* forget that this is *not* part of my lunch."

Chapter 4

The killer unlocked the garage door and entered the bloody room. The body had been cut up so soon after death there had not been time for the blood to clot. Blood was everywhere in the room. Paying no attention to it, the killer walked over to the freezer and stood next to it. *It's time to get rid of another body part. The old woman dumpster diver found the first body part just as I planned.*

Selecting a foot, the killer wrapped it. *Here goes another part of you. You bastard! It's going to be awhile before all of your body gets to be together in hell.*

Picking up the package, the mystery murderer left the garage and locked the door. After opening the passenger door, and tossing the package onto the seat, the killer went around to the driver's side, opened the door and stepped into the car. Ignition on and engine running, the red Ford Taurus sped quickly down the street.

During the trip to the dumpster, the killer glanced at the meticulously wrapped package on the seat. No one would suspect it was anything other than a beef roast. *You should be happy. You're going to meet another part of your body I've already given them.* A heinous laugh burst from twisted lips.

Suddenly, blue flashing lights reflected in the rear view mirror. The killer pulled the car over to the side of the road, heart pounding. The police car pulled up behind it and stopped.

Shit! Too late to try and hide it now.

Rolling down the window, the killer nonchalantly smiled and greeted the cop. "Hi officer, what'd you stop me for?"

The cop peered into the car and asked, "Do you know how fast you were going?"

"No, I was thinking of something," he said, sweat dripping down his forehead. "Was I going too fast?"

"Yeah, about ten miles over the speed limit," the cop replied as he bent his head and looked into the car at the package on the seat.

Let me see your license and proof of insurance."

I will gladly give them to you just so you'll go away. After digging through the glove compartment, he found the documents and handed them over.

"I'll be back in a minute." He went back to the cruiser. A few tortuous minutes later, he returned. "Okay, there are no warrants out for you. I'm going to let you go this time. Just a warning, slow down. Pay attention to your driving."

"Oh, thank you." The killer let out a huge breath of relief. "I will definitely watch my driving now."

When the cop pulled out and drove away, the killer sat back in the seat and took another big breath and let it out. *Thank God he didn't ask to see what's in the package.*

Continuing on, the killer drove to the dumpster site and waited for the garbage truck.

When it came and finally left, ten minutes passed to make sure no one happened to be in the vicinity of the dumpster then the Taurus pulled closer to it.

The killer picked up the package, exited the car and heaved it into the dumpster.

It dropped with a clunk into the empty container

The killer stood there looking down into the large receptacle with a feeling of partial satisfaction. *Take that, you son of a bitch. Each piece of you I throw in the trash will be another part of the hate I feel for you. You broke the trust I had in you into pieces. Every time, I am exacting a little more revenge for what you did to me.*

A multitude of feelings that led up to the victim's death descended on the killer as the dumpster lid closed. It started with passion, then sensitivity, awareness and finally anger. The murderer tried several times to control dangerous emotions. However, certain traits kept it from happening. Pride, ego and dignity topped the list.

While backing away from the dumpster, one of the loops on the killer's jeans caught on something sharp. It tore a jagged hole. *Damn it, just what I needed. Now I have to buy a new pair of jeans. I can't go to work in these.*

Loneliness overcame the killer on the drive home. *I wish my brother was still alive. I lost my best friend and defender when Sam died in that car accident. Only sixteen. He was in the prime of his life.*

A tear cascaded down the killer's face. *It's not fair. He was the only one who protected me when the kids at school picked on me.*

The butcher punched the steering wheel with a fist.

Entering the apartment, extreme agitation and bitterness brought about a violent emotional explosion. Trying to be as quiet as possible, the murderer took numerous items from the cabinets and refrigerator and splattered the contents out over the extremely clean kitchen counters. Then, the individual who murdered and butchered another human being, cuddled the dog.

Calmed at last, the killer sneaked into the dark bedroom, undressed and slid into bed next to the loving person who was sound asleep.

Chapter 5

Lee sat at his desk with one leg stretched out, the heel resting on a pile of papers. Cat perched on top of her meticulously neat desk.

Someone handed him a copy of the identity and address of the dumpster victim. He read it and jumped out of his chair. "That's the same address as a woman who filed a missing persons report. Her husband disappeared."

"Okay, let's go tell her we found him," said Cat. "This is going to be strange. We never told a wife we found *part* of her husband before."

They left their office and drove to an apartment complex in the southern part of Jamesburg. The building in which the victim's wife resided was constructed with three tan and white towers with peaked roofs. They obtained the correct apartment number at the manager's office and knocked on the door.

A slender woman in her early thirties opened the door only a crack.

Lee showed his badge as he asked, "Katrina Wolford?"

"Yes." The woman frowned. "This is about my husband isn't it? I reported him missing."

Cat answered, "I'm afraid it is. We're detectives from the Jamesburg police department. I'm sorry to tell you we've found your missing husband. He's been murdered."

She started weeping. "I knew it, I knew it! Ron always comes home right after work because I have dinner waiting for him. Last night he didn't even *come* home."

She closed her eyes and grabbed Cat's arm. "I'm feeling dizzy. I need to sit down. I don't understand who would want to kill Ron. Everyone liked him." Tears streaked down her cheeks as Cat helped her to a white couch in a tidy living room.

Lee pulled a chair from under a table that was next to a wall and sat down. Cat attempted to comfort the extremely upset woman. She violently drew in breaths and wailed as she released them.

"Is there any tissue I can get for you?" Cat asked.

Katrina stopped crying long enough to say, "Yes, there's some in the kitchen." She pointed to a small kitchen behind a half wall. Then, head in hands she started sobbing again.

While Cat was in the kitchen, Lee noticed a spiral staircase with a metal post in the middle leading to the second floor. He glanced around the room. It was lavishly furnished with white furniture, a white rug and huge expensive-looking paintings on the walls.

I wish my apartment looked like this. On second thought, it's too ritzy for me.

Cat returned and handed the woman a tissue. She waited a few minutes for her to regain a little composure, then asked, "Can you give us some information about you and your husband?"

Katrina stopped crying and after letting out a few large sighs, she replied, "My husband and I have been married for three years." She stopped, looked up and asked, "Can you tell me how he was killed? Do you know who killed him?"

Lee stood and said, "We don't know how he died yet. We've only found part of your husband's body. One of your husband's hands has been discovered."

The petite woman shrieked, "Oh, my God!" as she pushed her long blonde hair away from her face. "You mean someone murdered him then cut him up?"

"I'm afraid so," Lee replied.

"We have a newborn son," Katrina said, tears streaming down her face again. He's at my mom and dad's house right now. They've been taking care of him since Ron disappeared. I'm a stay-at-home mom, but I have been so worked up about Ron not coming home that I couldn't take care of him."

Lee told Katrina, "We are going to interview other residents of the building. When we know anything else, we'll let you know."

Lee and Cat left the distraught woman still sobbing.

Shortly after Lee and Cat left, Katrina heard a knock on her door.

Tall, lanky Victor Paulson and his red haired wife Angela stood at the doorway when she opened it.

Victor asked with concern in his voice, "Katrina, we saw the cops at your place. Why were they here?"

Katrina, still drying her tears, replied, "Vic, you guys shouldn't have come here so soon. What if the detectives saw you?"

"We don't care if they saw us. What were they doing here, anyway?"

"Ron's dead. Someone killed him and cut up his body. So far, they only found his hand."

Katrina fixed her eyes on Victor's astonished face. The long, slender features usually showing a gentle, kindhearted expression now showed a terse, no holds barred look.

"Holy shit! Somebody killed him?" He ran his fingers through his salt and pepper grey hair.

Angela's mouth dropped open. She gasped. "Why would somebody kill Ron?"

"I don't know, but the police are going to talk to other people in the apartments. You better go home. I don't want them to find you here."

Victor replied and stroked his grey beard, "It's okay. As far as anyone knows, we're all just friends."

Chapter 6

Immediately after Victor and Angela left Katrina's apartment, they knocked on Anita Carlson's door. Forty six year old, blonde haired, blue eyed Anita and her husband Joseph were also Ron's friends.

She answered the door with a smile on her face. "Hi guys, how are you?"

Angela, with a sad expression, took Anita's hand, "We just came from Katrina's. Two detectives told her that Ron is dead."

Anita's smile quickly disappeared. She seemed shocked at the news.

She abruptly dropped Angela's hand and exclaimed, "Oh, my God! No wonder I haven't heard from him for a couple of days. He was supposed to call me about something." Tears welled up in her eyes and ran down her cheeks, messing up her makeup. "Was he in an accident?"

"No, Katrina told us he was murdered," said Victor.

"What?" A horrified look came over her face. Her hands quickly went to her forehead. She pushed her long, blonde hair back and shook her head. "Why would anyone want to kill Ron? He was one of the nicest people I ever knew."

"We think he was too," Angela said. What's really appalling about it is they cut his body up and threw a hand in a dumpster."

Anita started sobbing. "How horrible! Why would somebody do that?"

They don't know who killed him yet. We thought his friends should know."

"Thanks for telling me," Anita replied, tears still

streaming down her face. "I'll call Hazel and tell her."

Hazel Sawyer and her husband Manny rounded out the group of Ron's friends.

The door no sooner closed behind Victor and Angela when Anita started sobbing uncontrollably. It took her awhile to calm down enough to call Hazel. "Hazel, meet me down at the pool in a few minutes. I have something to tell you. I'd have you come to the apartment, but Joseph might come home."

Anita took a few minutes to regain composure. She wiped tears from her eyes and reapplied makeup. Then, looking briefly into the mirror, took a deep breath, left the bathroom and the apartment.

She opened the door to the pool and noticed thirty two year old Hazel, sitting at one of the tan patio tables. Her short, brown hair looked a little messy as if she recently climbed out of bed without bothering to comb it. A glint in her big brown eyes and a wide smile signaled her happiness at seeing her friend.

Glancing around the large, rectangular pool area, Anita didn't see anyone else. There wasn't anyone sunbathing in any of the lounging chairs next to the tables. Satisfied no one could overhear what she was about to tell Hazel, she walked over and took a seat at her table. Anita was thankful large umbrellas at each table kept the sun at bay.

"It's about time you got here. What did you want to tell me?"

Anita took in a sizable breath. "Victor and Angela just came to my apartment and told me Ron is dead. He was murdered." Tears welled up in her eyes again.

"Jesus, why would someone murder Ron? He was such a good guy," Hazel said as she teared up.

"They don't know why. They haven't caught the killer yet." Closing her eyes for a few seconds and drawing in a large breath, Anita said, "There's something else I have to tell you."

Hazel looked puzzled with Anita's crying. "Okay, there's more than Ron's murder going on here. What is it? Tell me."

"Whoever murdered Ron threw one of his hands in a dumpster."

"Holy shit! You mean they cut him into pieces?"

"Yes. They haven't found the rest of his body yet." Anita nervously shifted in her chair. "There's something else I want to tell you, but you have to promise not to tell anyone else."

Hazel put her hand on Anita's arm. "You know I wouldn't tell anyone else if you asked me not to. What is it that's so secretive?"

"Ron and I had been seeing each other for awhile. I loved him and he loved me."

"What? Oh my God, Anita. It could have been Joseph or Katrina who killed him if one of them found out about it. If Katrina didn't kill him herself, she may have hired someone to do it. Somehow, I can't think of Katrina actually cutting up his body. It could have been Joseph. I know how jealous he was of other men. But I've known Joseph long enough to find it hard to believe it could have been him. He's just not the type of person to do something like that."

Suddenly Anita heard a noise from behind one of the tables and stood up. "My God, Hazel! Someone's sunbathing on a lounge chair hidden by the table. I didn't know she was there."

The sunbather, a woman, stood and walked over to Anita and Hazel's table.

Anita whispered to Hazel, "It's Tamara Garrett."

Tamara was a young resident of their apartment building. Anita guessed she was probably in her late twenties or early thirties. She also knew Tamara came on to most of the men in the apartment building. She didn't care if they were married or not. They all seemed to be fair game.

Tamara didn't wait for an invitation to sit down. She plopped herself into one of the chairs at the table. "I overheard everything. I heard Anita tell you about Ron's death and also about their affair. I truly feel bad about Ron being murdered. But Anita, you shouldn't have any anxiety about your affair with him. I have affairs with married men all the time. You'd be surprised how many men are willing to have clandestine affairs even if they love their wives."

Anita looked at her and frowned. "I didn't know you overheard us. It's none of your business. Come on Hazel, let's go."

Hazel replied, "Wait a minute. You haven't told me anything about the affair. She already knows about it, so you might as well tell her too.

"Yes, I want to hear about it," Tamara said as she twisted a lock of her long, dark brown hair and raised her eyebrows to make her brown eyes larger.

Anita thought about it for a few minutes. Then she agreed since she figured Hazel would probably tell her about it anyway. "Okay, but if you tell anyone else, I'll deny it."

"I promise."

"One day Ron came to our apartment while Joseph was at work. He said Joseph told him he could borrow a book he wanted to read. While I was trying to find it, one thing led to another and we ended up kissing. The next day, he came back and we had sex. Katrina was about to have a baby and Ron felt pretty horny. I had been feeling quite neglected by Joseph. It was just casual sex at first. Then we both started having feelings for each other. Just before Ron died, we both knew we loved each other. We talked about leaving our spouses, but Ron was murdered before we could."

Tamara stood and gave Anita a hug. "I'm so sorry Ron died before you had the chance to be together."

Anita, astonished by Tamara's reaction, replied, "Thank you Tamara. That means a lot to me."

Tamara looked over at Hazel and noticed she was crying. "Hazel, I know you and Ron were friends too. Come on over here and let's have a group hug."

Hazel quickly went over to the other two women and they gathered together and hugged as one entity.

When Anita left the group, she was confused about her opinion of Tamara since she showed sympathy for the two older women. She noticed Hazel still crying over Ron's murder.

Chapter 7

Two days after Maggie found a man's hand behind a Safeway store, she decided to try a dumpster at another strip mall. This time she chose one behind the Dollar store. The dumpster stood against the back wall. An unpaved road separated the store from a forested area which Maggie heard was part of the woods where she lived in the homeless camp.

Breakfast seemed like a lifetime ago. A few peanut butter filled crackers wasn't enough for lunch. Hunger pangs drove her to open the dumpster at nine P.M. She looked cautiously inside the huge metal container and shined her mini flashlight inside.

"Holy cow! Looks like I hit da jackpot dis time."

She could see a box of Honey Buns, a large can of peanuts and a bag of chocolate chip cookies. Other items peeked out from under the food already in her line of sight, but she couldn't make out what they were

"Dis makes up for da horrible results of da other dumpster."

When she finished placing the first three objects into her cart, she returned to the dumpster hoping to find other edible items.

The awful find she made at the other dumpster now seemed like a dream.

Maggie resumed digging into the contents of what appeared to be the ultimate goal of any dumpster diver. She uncovered enough food to last her quite a few days.

"Wow, dis is fantastic," she said as she found a jar of strawberry preserves and a box of crackers. A can of black olives came into sight. "If I kin find something to go with dese, I'll have a good lunch today." Then she remembered, "I already found some cheese a couple days ago. Olives, crackers and cheese go prurty good together."

To top it off, she found a whole pecan pie.

As she decided she found enough to last a few days, something near the bottom of the dumpster caught her eye. Wrapped in foil, it looked like it might possibly be a piece of meat. This package captured Maggie's interest.

"What da heck could dis be?"

Curiosity took precedence over interest. She found a wooden box in the alley and placed it next to the dumpster. Standing on her tiptoes, she bent and reached as far as possible. It took a while, but she finally snagged the package.

"I hope dis is worth it."

Maggie raised the package to her nose and sniffed it. "It doesn't smell spoilt."

As she carefully unwrapped the foil, a portion of the contents protruded from it.

A human toe!

The astounded woman shrieked and dropped the package. It fell on the ground next to the dumpster.

"Dis can't be happenen to me agin."

She began to tremble. She looked up and down the alley both ways. No one was in sight. Choosing her only option, she ran around the building to the parking lot.

Maggie noticed a man stepping out of his car and ran up to him. Still ruffled, she could hardly speak. "Call da police!" The man sat down in his car again and looked bewildered. She pounded on his car and screamed, "Call da police! I just found part of a body in da dumpster."

He immediately dialed 911.

As they waited for the police to arrive, the man tried to calm her down. She told him about the other body part she found.

The first officer to arrive on the scene took one look at the woman who found the body part and asked, "Say, aren't you the homeless lady who found another body part in a dumpster the other day?"

"Yes! I can't believe I found another one. I know it looks bad for me, but I swear I din't do it."

"It seems like quite a coincidence to me. I think we should check you out better this time. Show me the body part you found."

Maggie took the cop to the foil-wrapped package lying on the ground next to the dumpster. After acknowledging it was authentic, he took her to the police car and locked her in the back seat.

"You stay here until the detectives get here. They are definitely going to want to talk to you."

Then he returned to the dumpster and placed yellow crime scene tape around the area. As he finished the taping, several other police cars arrived.

The distressed bag lady cried as she waited in the back of the police car. "Why is dis happenin' to me?"

Chapter 8

Cat and Lee finished their dinner and stood in line to pay when Lee's phone rang. As he listened to the dispatcher, his expression changed from a relaxed state to that of extreme interest.

When he hung up, he turned to her. "We gotta go! Someone found a foot in a dumpster."

"Sounds like they found another part of our victim."

Lee shoved a TicTac into his mouth and said, "Yeah, the killer's been busy."

"No more parts of the victim were found in any of the dumpsters in the city. That means he disposed of the foot since then."

"The body must be getting pretty rancid by now."

"Unless he froze the body."

As they drove to the scene, Lee marveled at what a beautiful place he lived in for the last three years. Tall dark green fir trees rose like high rise buildings in downtown Seattle. Their fresh smell enhanced the air, unlike the air in Detroit.

He pointed and asked Cat, "See those two hawks sitting on that light post?"

"Yes, they probably have young ones nearby."

"That's something you don't see in Detroit."

"Would you ever consider living in a big city again?"

"Never!"

When the two detectives arrived at the Dollar store, a small crowd already milled around outside the crime scene tape.

Maggie, still in the back seat of the police car, hoped they would talk to her soon. Tears no longer streamed down her face, but she remained visibly shaken.

The first objective for Cat and Lee presented itself as they rounded the corner of the building. The first officer on the scene showed them the foil wrapped package on the ground next to the dumpster.

Cat put some gloves on. After she and Lee gave the package a quick look over, they sent it to be checked for fingerprints and then on to the Medical Examiner.

Then they turned their attention to Maggie McGraw. An officer transferred her to Lee and Cat's car.

Cat began the conversation. "Maggie, it seems like a weird coincidence that you are the person that found both parts of the victim's body."

"I know. Ya gotta believe me, I din't kill him. How can I prove to ya dat I din't do it?"

"Well, there's one way you could do that. You could take a lie detector test."

"I'll do it! You'll see I din't kill dat man."

One of the police officers took Maggie to the police station to wait for the lie detector analyst to arrive.

When they watched the police car leave with Maggie, Cat turned, raised her eyebrows and said with a smile, "Are you up to a little dumpster diving, Lee?"

"What?"

"I think we should dive into this dumpster ourselves and see what we find. Hopefully, we will find more body parts. Who knows what we'll find."

"Are you kidding? You actually want *us* to get into that dumpster and rummage around?"

"Yep, you and your clothes are washable. You can take a nice warm shower when you get home. I think it'll be fun."

"If I do this, I'm going to take a *scorching hot shower* when I get home."

"Okay then, let's get started."

"Do you have a clothespin to put on my nose?"

They both donned rubber gloves. Cat led the way, jumping onto the wooden box Maggie used to get into the dumpster. Once she was in the dumpster, she yelled, "Get in too!"

"I can't believe I'm doing this." He climbed into the dumpster also.

Neither found more body parts, nor anything to help with the case.

Lee exclaimed, "My God that stuff stinks. How are we going to go home in these? We'll stink up the car."

Gothcha covered. The Dollar store sells long raincoats. I know. I bought one there a couple weeks ago. We can take our shoes off and put them on newspaper in the trunk."

"I think I'll throw mine away. I'll never get the smell out of them. How in the hell do dumpster divers do this all the time?"

"Most of them come prepared."

"Thank you for letting me know this now."

Chapter 9

Lee and Cat received the results of Maggie's lie detector test. Then they drove to tell Mrs. Wolford someone discovered another part of her husband's body. Their plans also included interviewing residents at the same apartment complex.

Cat said, "Well, it looks like Maggie isn't our killer. She passed the lie detector test. It sure is strange though that she is the one who found both of the body parts. What a coincidence."

"Maybe she knows the killer and he knows where her favorite dumpsters are," Lee remarked.

"How would he know which dumpster she's going to dig in next?"

"I don't know," Lee replied, "but let's see if she has a routine. Maybe he knows what days she goes to each one. Let's talk to Maggie after we're done interviewing the residents at the apartment building."

When they arrived at the apartment complex, everything appeared to be back to normal. The hubbub that their presence caused when they met with Katrina Wolford was no longer evident. By now, everyone seemed to know about Ron Wolford's murder.

When Katrina answered the door, Lee and Cat could see she still grieved for her husband. Dressed in pajamas and a robe, her eyelids looked swollen and she held a tissue to her nose. They guessed she had not been out since learning of her husband's death. Parts of her hair looked uncombed and tangled.

"We're sorry to disturb you Mrs. Wolford," Cat said, "but we told you we'd keep you posted when anything new happened concerning your husband's murder. We want you to know that someone found one of your husband's feet in a dumpster."

Katrina became extremely upset and began to cry. "Why is my husband's killer dumping his body a little at a time? I hope you catch this freak soon. I wish they could do the same thing to him."

"We are doing everything we can to find who it is," said Lee. "Believe me, we want to catch the killer as much as you do. We're here to interview other people who live here. We'll keep you abreast of any new developments."

When they left the Wolford apartment, Lee and Cat began questioning other residents. The first tenant they questioned lived next door to Katrina and Ron Wolford. A married couple lived in the apartment. A woman answered the door.

"My husband is at work. We heard about Ron. What an awful thing."

"We want to talk to both you and your husband, but can you answer a couple of questions now?" Lee asked.

"Yes, of course."

"Do you know the Wolfords?"

"We don't know them very well. We met them several times at parties the apartment managers threw."

"Do you know," Cat asked, "of any reason someone would want to kill Mr. Wolford?"

"He seemed like such a nice person. I don't know why anyone would want to kill him. He and his wife seemed to get along really well."

"Let us know when we can talk to both of you. In the meantime, if you hear of anything at all, contact us."

Lee and Cat tried the apartment on the other side of the Wolford's, but no one answered the door. They left a card on the door asking the occupants to call them. Then they knocked on the door of the apartment two doors down from the Wolford's apartment.

It looked like the woman who answered the door had been crying. She wiped her eyes with a tissue and then, blowing her nose, asked, "Can I help you?"

Cat, placing a hand on the woman's shoulder, asked, "Are you okay?"

The woman laughed and replied, "I'm fine. I just watched a sad movie on TV.

"I'm Lee Cummings and this is Catherine Hendrix. We are with the Jamesburg police department. You've probably heard that Ron Wolford has been murdered."

"Yes, I heard. Is it true that his body was horribly dismembered?"

"I'm afraid it was. Can we ask you a couple of questions? Are you up to that?"

"I am. Okay, I'm Anita Carlson and my husband's name is Joseph."

"Did you know Ron Wolford?" Cat asked.

"Yes, my husband and I both knew him. We knew both he and his wife. We've been to each other's homes a lot."

"Did Mr. Wolford and his wife appear to be happily married? Did they argue?"

"They seemed to be. There were never any arguments when we were with them."

"Do you know of anyone who might want to kill Mr. Wolford? Anyone in the area?"

Tears welled up in her eyes again. "No, I have no idea who would want to kill him. He was a wonderful man. I don't know anyone who would want him dead. What kind of monster could cut his body into pieces?"

"When your husband comes home," said Lee, "have him call us."

At the next apartment, both the husband and wife were home. They welcomed Lee and Cat into their home and offered them something to drink.

The wife said, "We'd like to tell you something we know. We don't have any idea if it has anything to do with Ron's murder, but we think you should know it."

"Whatever it is," Lee said, "we want to know it so we can find out if it is connected to our case."

The husband said with reservation in his voice, "This is something we have heard several times." He took a deep breath and with his wife holding his hand, he continued, "We heard that Ron Wolford and his wife are, or were, swingers. Supposedly, there are several swinger couples living in the apartment complex. We also heard that Anita and Joseph Carlson are swingers too. That's the only names we know, but we heard there are several more swinger couples here."

They thanked the couple and stepped outside.

"Holy shit, what's going on here?" Lee exclaimed. Let's take a break to figure out what our next move should be.

"We need to find out," Cat said, "who all of the swingers are. The chances are Ron Wolford knew the person who killed him. It's possible one of them is the nasty killer."

"I agree. Let's start with Katrina Wolford. She seemed to be suffering a lot of grief. If she doesn't know who killed her husband, she may be tempted to give us names of everyone of the swingers to help find the killer."

When they went to Katrina's apartment, they found her still in the same pajamas and robe as when they spoke with her earlier. Puffy eyes and a sniffling nose told them she truly grieved for him. Lee and Cat realized that she probably didn't kill him, but would she give them the names of the other swingers?

Lee began the interrogation of Katrina. "Mrs. Wolford, we know that you and your husband were part of a group of swingers. We need the names of everyone in the group."

An astounded expression came over Katrina's face. "What makes you think something like that?"

"Don't try to deny it," Cat said in a firm voice. "There are some residents in the apartment building that know what's going on here."

Katrina backed up and sat down in one of the huge chairs that matched the white couch.

She burst out crying, covered her face with her hands and said, "I don't know what to say except that Ron and I loved each other very much. We met this other couple and spent a lot of time with them. They are the ones who eventually got us into the group. We had never done anything like that before. We haven't done anything with the group since we had the baby. Please don't think bad of us. We talked about leaving the group before Ron was murdered." Katrina shook too much to talk. She lowered her head, put her face in her hands and sobbed uncontrollably.

Cat went over to her and bent down. "Take your time, Katrina. We're not here to judge you. That's something that will be done by a higher power than any of us. What we want from you is the names of the other couples in your group. We think your husband might have been killed by someone he knew. It could be someone from the group."

"I can't believe it could be someone we know. They all seem so friendly. I don't know what reason any of them would have for killing him.

"We don't know if any of them are guilty of killing your husband," Cat said. "They are all possible suspects. We need the names and apartment numbers of everyone in the group."

Katrina pulled herself together enough to give them

a list of names. Including Ron and Katrina, there were eight members of the group. The first names on the list were Katrina and Ron's closest friends, Victor and Angela Paulson.

After Lee and Cat left Katrina, they headed for the Paulons. Victor Paulson answered the door. He looked to be in his thirties. Blue eyes and light brown hair topped off a tall slender body.

"We're interviewing residents of the building concerning Ron Wolford's death," said Lee.

Victor's petite, red haired wife joined him. She stood beside him and wrapped her arm around his waist.

Cat continued. "We understand you are friends with Ron and Katrina Wolford. I'm sure you've heard Ron was murdered."

Victor replied, "Yes, I can't believe he's dead."

Angela added, "We heard whoever killed him dismembered him too. Is that true?"

"Yes, I'm afraid that's true," replied Cat. "We think someone he knew may have killed him."

Victor took a step back and with a look of panic. "You don't think we did it do you?"

"Right now, we are only interviewing people he knew," Lee responded. "Katrina told us you were their friends."

"Did she tell you anything else?"

Cat, holding back a smirk, replied, "As a matter of fact, she did. She gave us a list of swingers and you two are on the list. However, we already knew it before we talked to her."

"How did you know that?" Angela asked.

"Some of the other residents are aware of your swingers group."

When they finished interviewing the Paulsons, Lee and Cat returned to Anita and Joseph Carlson's apartment. Joseph Carlson called them while they were at the Paulson's to let them know he'd arrived home.

Joseph Carlson's dark hair and thin dark mustache made him look like quite a heartthrob.

Cat thought, *I imagine he's pretty popular in the swinger group.*

His wife's puffy eyes had been replaced with makeup that looked like it had been done by a professional. Her blonde hair, perfectly curled and combed, looked like she could walk onto any movie set as the star.

Anita introduced her husband to Lee and Cat, "This is my husband, Joe. I told him you were interviewing the residents in the building about Ron's murder."

Lee came right to the point. "We're here because we think someone who knew Ron killed him. We know you both knew him and his wife. We were also apprised of the fact that both of you and Ron and Katrina were swingers."

A shocked look came over Anita's face. She frowned and said, "Who told you that? Was it Katrina?"

"Actually, a number of people told us. Your names came up while they were talking about it," Cat said in a matter of fact tone.

Anita said, "It's not true!"

Joseph laid one hand on his wife's shoulder and said, "There's no use lying about it Anita, it'll probably be all through the apartment complex in a few days." Turning to Cat, he asked, "Are we suspects?"

"You and everyone in the swinger group are possible murder suspects."

Anita never said another word the whole time Lee and Cat talked to Joseph.

The last couple on the list was Hazel and Manny Sawyer. Lee and Cat headed there next.

Hazel answered the door. Lee and Cat introduced

themselves, then started to ask questions.

"Who is it Hazel?" asked Manny from a room down the hall.

"It's a couple of detectives about Ron's murder."

"What the hell do they want? We don't know nothing about it."

"They just want to ask a few questions."

Manny Sawyer, a short stocky man with light brown hair, who looked to be in his thirties or forties, appeared and shoved his wife aside. "Don't answer any questions."

Turning to the detectives he said, "You hard of hearin? I said we don't know nothing about his murder. So just leave us alone."

"Fine, we'll send a couple of cops to bring you to the station," said Lee. "We can ask you questions there as well as here."

Both detectives turned and walked down the steps. As they entered the car, Lee whispered, "Dumb shit! We'll do it his way."

Chapter 10

Victor, essentially the leader of the group, called Joseph. "I think the members of the group should all get together. We should discuss everything concerning Ron's death and the fact that the cops know we are swingers."

"Yeah," Joseph said, "I think so too. Let's have a swingers pool party. Katrina needs something to help her get over Ron's death."

"Okay, sounds good. Why don't you let everyone know. I'll get everything ready for the party."

When Victor finished talking to Joseph, he called the manager of the apartments. "I'm having a pool party in a little while and would like to have the pool closed for the rest of the day if possible."

"All right, I'll go down, clear out anyone down there and put a sign on the door. I'll lock it up and bring you the key."

A short time later he dropped the key off at Victor's apartment.

Victor made a quick trip to the grocery store to pick up finger food for the party since there was no time for preparation. He and Angela already had enough drinks on hand for the whole group.

After returning from the store, he set out the food and drinks at the pool. He also brought enough large-sized bath towels for each of the group.

When everything was set up, Victor called Joseph. "Everything's ready for the party. Tell everyone to come down to the pool."

Joseph called all of the other members of the group. When everyone had congregated poolside, Victor closed the door and locked it. The entire group wore skimpy and revealing bathing suits. They sat down at two tables Victor had pulled together. A delectable array of treats greeted them. They passed the food around and thoroughly enjoyed the meal.

While they ate, Victor said, "I'd like to know who told the police we're swingers."

Katrina responded with a disagreeable look on her face. "What difference does it make? They can't arrest us for being swingers. I just want them to find out who killed Ron."

"Speaking of Ron," Joseph asked, "Do they have any leads as to who killed him?"

Katrina replied, "Not yet. I hope they catch somebody soon."

"Huh!" Manny said, showing a disgusted look. "They want to interview *me* down at the police station because I told them to get lost. I'm surprised they *don't* arrest us for being swingers. I say piss on them." Manny's view of society as a whole was different than the other group members.

Victor stated, "They think it's probably somebody he knew. That means, it *could* be one of us."

"It also means it could be a man *or* a woman," Katrina said, looking around at everyone at the table.

"Yeah," Angela said, it could even be *you*."

Victor pushed his chair back and said, "Okay! Okay! Let's just drop it for the time being. We're here to have a good time. Katrina needs our support right now and Ron wouldn't us to be unhappy. He'd want a celebration of his life instead."

He stood and announced, "I thought we could start out by playing a game of Twister."

Everyone agreed it would be a good way to kick the party off. Victor picked up and spread out a plastic mat with six rows of large colored circles on it with a different color in each row. Then he picked up a square board with a spinner on it.

"Normal games consist of someone spinning the spinner and telling the players to put their hand or foot on a color," said Victor. "These people are totally dressed. However, with we swingers, each spin determines which article of clothing we'll take off and which color to put a hand or foot on. Also, during the game, the players can kiss or fondle whoever they want to."

During the game, Anita looked at Victor and said, "Ooh, I see someone's already horny."

Victor replied, "Maybe you can remedy that."

"I am looking forward to doing that," Anita uttered in a low, sexy voice."

Manny fondled Katrina's breasts, larger than they used to be because of the baby. "Too bad these won't stay this way," he quipped.

She replied, "No, but you can have fun with them until they change."

"The fun's just starting," Hazel said as she leaned over and kissed Joseph.

The game went on until every swinger was completely undressed. When the game ended, the mood had changed. Each member of the group appeared to be in high spirits.

Hazel shouted, "Let's play a game of Chicken Fight in the pool."

"What's Chicken Fight?" asked Hazel.

"Chicken Fight is a game where someone jumps on somebody else's shoulders and tries to knock their opponents into the water."

A big cheer went up and everyone raced to the pool. There was no need to remove their bathing suits since everyone was already undressed. They all whooped and jumped into the pool.

Katrina's baby was still at her parent's home. It gave her the freedom to enjoy herself. She had already lost most of her baby fat. She had such a great looking female physique, men would be ringing her doorbell soon. She jumped on Hazel's shoulders.

Victor started splashing water onto Angela who was on Joseph's back. Angela was usually a very quiet, reserved person. However, on this day, she was not. She jumped on Manny's shoulders and started trying to push Katrina off Hazel's shoulders.

When they finished playing Chicken Fight, everyone jumped into the Jacuzzi and then played footsie with each other. After awhile, they switched places on the Jacuzzi seat. They discussed the fun that was still to come. Everyone was anticipating what they were going to do to have an exciting finish to the evening.

Midway through the revelry, Manny announced, "Sorry to leave the fun, but I have to go to work. Be sure to lock the door after me unless you're going take the next phase of the night to one of your apartments." He took one last look at the group's merriment and remarked, "Two men and four women should be lots of fun."

Chapter 11

The day after the pool party, Manny called Lee and talked to him about the interview. "You don't need to send the cops to take me to the station," he said. I'll come myself. I thought it over and decided it might be in my best interest to give in to you detectives."

Manny drove up to the police station at precisely the time they agreed on. He had chosen to calm down his temperament a little. He would be as nice to the detectives as possible. However, it wasn't long before he became irritated. He waited a half hour for Lee and Cat to even get to the station.

"Sorry we're late," said Lee. "We had something else related to the case we had to do first.

Yeah right. You suckers kept me waiting here on purpose. Manny mumbled, "It's okay. Let's just do it"

The interview started out quiet and peaceful. Manny sat down at a table across from Lee and Cat.

Lee started, "We are going to record this interview."

"Okay, If ya have to."

Lee turned on the recorder. "Would you please state your full name for the record."

"Yah, it's Manny Sawyer."

"How old are you Manny?"

"I'm thirty seven."

"Give us your address."

Manny quietly gave them his address.

"What do you do for a living?"

Manny nervously uncrossed his legs and crossed them to the other side of his body. "I'm a butcher for Crawford meats."

Lee and Cat looked at each other with a sudden

uptake in their interest for what Manny was telling them.

Cat asked, "How long have you worked for them?"

"About three years. Hesitating for a few seconds, he asked, "Does it really make a difference how long I've worked for 'em?"

"We just need it for the record," Cat replied.

Lee asked, "What were you doing the night Ron Wolford disappeared?"

"I was working," he answered , uncrossing his legs.

"Were you friends with the Wolfords?" Lee inquired.

Somewhat agitated, Manny responded, "I heard you already know my wife and me are swingers. So I reckon you should already know we're well acquainted with the Wolfords."

Lee held his hand up. "Take it easy Manny. We're just trying to find out things that could be important to this investigation."

"I *do* think it's interesting that Ron's body was cut up and you just happen to be a butcher," Cat told him in a very matter of fact tone.

"I don't care how interesting a couple of hot shot detectives think it is. I haven't done anything wrong. I didn't cut up Ron's body and I sure as hell didn't kill him."

"We didn't say you did, Manny," Lee said raising his voice slightly, trying not to sound harsh. "You can't blame us for thinking it sounds strange that you are a butcher when Ron's body was cut into pieces."

"So, am I a suspect?"

Cat answered, "Only until we corroborate where you were on the night Ron disappeared."

Manny rose out of the chair so fast he knocked it over. "I haven't killed anyone! You're just like all the cops I ever knew of." He raised his hand, made a fist and shook it at Lee and Cat. "You all think people are guilty until you prove them innocent. We're supposed to be innocent until you prove us guilty."

He appeared to be taller than five feet at the moment. Cat realized he probably tried to make up for being short by having a raging temper.

Manny turned and shouted, "You all go to hell. This interview is over!

After Manny left, Lee said, "Wow, that guy's got a lot of anger in him. I wonder if he's like that with all the other swingers?"

Cat responded, "Yeah, he's got quite a temper. We'll see if he's still a suspect when we check to find out if he was actually working or not on the night when Ron disappeared."

"But," Lee came back with, "what if he killed him earlier in the day? We need to find out if Ron went to work that day. If he did, maybe he got off early enough so Manny was able to kill him before he went to work. There's lots of 'ifs' here."

Cat agreed. "Too many loose ends."

Chapter 12

The killer, aware the police had been to the apartment building interviewing people, began to exhibit signs of anxiety. Thoughts raced. A quickened heart beat gave rise to nausea and a dizzy feeling. Frequent nightmares interrupted sleep.

Time came to dispose of another body part. Dread made eyes sting from beads of sweat rolling down the forehead.

A dumpster behind the Grocery Outlet store had been chosen as the next dump site. This time, it seemed a little harder to decide which body part to choose. The freezer opened once more. The victim's head seemed like a good choice. However, surveying the options left, several parts appeared to be better. When lifted, it was too heavy. The best choices seemed to be another hand or foot. Everything else was either too big or too awkward. The torso, definitely too big. The legs, too awkward. The head, too heavy.

"I already pitched a hand and a foot. I want to throw something different in the dumpster this time."

Going back over the parts left, the killer chose one awkward leg. Easy to carry, it seemed to be the best selection. The leg was packaged and put back into the freezer until time to go.

Getting more nervous with each passing minute, a little irritability was tacked on.

"Damn it, why does time go so slow when you're waiting for it to pass?"

Pacing up and down the garage sized building, time dragged on.

"Relax! Pacing won't make it go faster."

The time to go finally arrived.

"Thank God! I feel like I'm about to explode."

Opening the freezer lid, the killer, dressed in dark clothing, extracted the packaged leg and put it in the trunk of the car.

"Am I forgetting anything?"

Nothing seemed to be missing after walking back into the building and glancing around the room several times. "I've got everything."

The killer, now extremely nervous, backed out of the driveway and almost hit a passing car. Coming to a screeching halt inches from hitting the car, the driver slumped over the steering wheel, trembling from fright.

"What if I'd had an accident with the leg in the car? They might have caught me. I have to be more careful from now on."

A deep breath aided in finally backing the rest of the way out of the driveway. Driving more careful, it seemed to take forever to get to the Grocery Outlet store.

Upon arrival to the back of the store near the dumpster, it was almost time for the trash pickup. A steady breeze blew and the rustle of the trees annoyed the tense driver.

"Is that trash truck ever going to get here?"

When it finally arrived, the loud noise from emptying the Grocery store dumpster meant the time to throw the leg into it was getting close. Tension from waiting for the trash truck to empty dumpsters from two stores next to the Grocery Outlet became extreme.

"Come on! Come on! Damn it, why are you so slow getting here?"

The truck disappeared around the corner of the building after emptying the Grocery Outlet dumpster.

It seemed no one was around after checking the

area for anyone who might observe someone throwing something into the dumpster.

The killer opened the car trunk. A package containing the leg was removed. Not much more than a split second later, a dark shadow appeared on the wall of the building.

"Shit!" the killer exclaimed and dropped the leg.

Crouched behind the back of the car, frozen in fear, the killer slowly raised up. Then, realized the shadow came from a tree slightly past the end of the building. The wind blew the branches over enough to cast a shadow on the wall.

Letting out a sigh of relief, the pathetic person picked up the package and proceeded to the dumpster. Raising the dumpster cover, the killer heaved the leg into it.

"That's what you deserve, you bastard. I've got more of you to throw into the garbage because that's what you are. Garbage!"

Unexpectedly the wretched human being turned around and spied Manny Sawyer standing in the shadows.

"What'd you put in the dumpster?"

"Just some trash we decided to get rid of. What are you doing here?"

"I followed you. I know you killed Ron Wolford. I also know you have been throwing parts of Ron's body in dumpsters."

"What do you want? Are you thinking of blackmailing me or are you going to call the cops?"

"First, I want to see what you threw in the dumpster," Manny said as he pulled out a gun. He pointed it at the killer as he walked over to the dumpster and looked inside. Still pointing the gun, he reached into the dumpster. The package was too far down in the empty container.

"I can't reach it." Manny motioned with the pistol. "Get me something to stand on."

The killer found a wood box and gave it to him. Manny climbed on the box and still pointing the gun, looked away for a split second into the dumpster. Suddenly Manny was knocked off the box. He didn't have a chance to pull the trigger. A switchblade jabbed into his stomach as he fell. The gun dropped from his hand and clattered on the pavement.

"You son of a bitch!" Manny shouted as he landed on the ground.

A struggle ensued. Manny fought for his life. He noticed blood seeping from the wound to his stomach. Terrified, he grabbed the gun. However, the person who stabbed him also had a grasp on it. Manny managed to wrench it free and pointed it at his attacker. He was unable to shoot before the assailant pulled the knife out of his stomach and stabbed him again. The gun dropped from Manny's hand.

He put his hand up to try and grab the knife, but the blade went through the middle of his hand.

He screamed.

The knife was pulled quickly from his hand and he was stabbed several more times in the chest and stomach in rapid succession.

"Die! You son of a bitch!"

Manny lay silent and unmoving. The killer checked for a pulse.

None.

The killer picked up Manny's body and threw him into the dumpster. Blood in the alley was cleaned up from supplies stashed in the car trunk. Exhausted and shaken, the killer went through several scenarios of what to do next while driving home.

Chapter 13

Katrina Wolford arranged a closed casket funeral for Ron. She invited every resident of the apartment complex. Since residents attended the apartment parties, everyone knew him.

When Katrina went to Manny and Hazel's apartment to invite them to the funeral, Hazel answered the door in tears. She was shaking uncontrollably.

"Hazel, what's the matter?"

"Manny went somewhere really late last night and he hasn't come home yet."

"Did he tell you where he was going?"

"No, he just said not to expect him home until sometime this morning. Morning has come and gone and he's not home yet."

"Have you tried calling him on his cell phone?"

"Yes, he doesn't answer. He has always answered his cell phone whenever I call him. I'm really worried. I have no idea where he went, so I don't know where to start looking."

"Let's get in touch with the other members of our group. Maybe they know where he is."

"Okay, will you go to their apartments with me?"

"Yes, let's start at Victor and Angela's apartment."

Katrina knocked on Victor and Angela's door. Angela answered it. She looked surprised to see Katrina and Hazel.

"What are you guys doing here?"

"Hazel's husband seems to have disappeared."

Hazel, with tears in her eyes, said, "He left late last night and still isn't home. Do you or Vic know where he might have gone?"

"I have no idea. Vic will be home in about an hour. I'll ask him if he knows. Do you want to come in and have some coffee?"

"No, I better get home in case Manny shows up and wonders where I am."

They stopped at Joe and Anita's apartment. Joe took one look at Hazel's red, swollen eyes and asked, "Hey what's up?"

"Manny left late last night and still isn't home," Hazel replied. "He's never been late."

"Oh my God, Hazel," Joe said. "Do you know where he went?"

"No he didn't tell me where he was going. Do you know? Please tell me if you do."

"He didn't tell me he was going anywhere. Why don't you come in and we'll talk about it."

"I need to get home in case he shows up. He may already be there."

"Alright, but if he doesn't get home soon, why don't you come back and we'll get together with Katrina, Vic and Angela and see if we can figure something out. We all need to stick together."

"Okay, if he doesn't come home in the next couple of hours, we'll do that."

Katrina accompanied Hazel to her apartment. Hazel unlocked the door and called out, "Manny are you here?"

No answer!

Hazel started crying and asked Katrina, "Will you stay here with me for awhile?"

"Yes, of course I will." Katrina sat down on the sofa and asked, "Did Manny take anything with him?"

"No, not that I know of."

"Did he call anybody before he left?"

"No, unless he called them after he got in the car."

Hazel glanced at her watch. "It's late in the afternoon.

I haven't had any lunch, would you like something to eat? I can fix us something quick."

"Yes, I think as soon as we eat, if Manny isn't home, we should get us all together and see if we can figure out what to do."

While they ate, Katrina called Vic and Angela and Joe and Anita. Everyone agreed to meet at Hazel and Manny's apartment. Everyone tried to comfort Hazel when they arrived. Manny was still not home. Victor suggested that Hazel try to call Manny's cell phone again. She called him, but there was still no answer.

Angela said, "Maybe he's been in an accident. I think we should call the hospital."

Hazel dialed the hospital. After being on hold a minute, a pleasant sounding voice answered. "Jamesburg Hospital. How may I direct your call?"

"Could you tell me if a Manny Sawyer has been admitted to the hospital?"

"Just a moment, I'll check." There was a brief silence. "No, there is no record of a patient by that name being admitted to the hospital."

Katrina said, "I hate to say this. Maybe he left you. Have you checked to see if any of his clothes are gone?"

Hazel and Katrina checked the closet. None of his clothes appeared to be gone.

The group spent at least an hour trying to think of reasons why Manny had disappeared.

Unable to come up with any good ideas, Katrina said, "It's getting late. After what happened to Ron, I think it's time to call the police. The person that killed Ron may have killed Manny too."

Victor agreed. "Something is definitely wrong. If we call the police, I think we should all stay here. They are going to want to talk with each of us."

Hazel placed the call to the police. "Jamesburg police

department, how can I help you?"

"My husband, Manny Sawyer is missing. Could I speak to someone about it?"

"How long has he been missing?"

"Since late last night."

"I'm sorry. You can file a missing persons report if you wish."

Victor took the phone from Hazel and said, "Manny's disappearance might be connected to Ron Wolford's murder. You need to send Lee Cummings and Catherine Hendrix over here. They are the detectives investigating the Wolford case."

Only a few minutes lapsed before Lee Cummings called Hazel. Approximately half an hour later, Lee and Cat arrived at Hazel's apartment.

Chapter 14

The sun sent blistering rays raining down on Jamesburg. The temperature reached the mid nineties. Maggie tried to put the events of the past few days behind her as she sought shelter from the heat that plagued the city. She stayed in the middle of the wooded area behind the Safeway store most of the day. The large fir trees offered some protection from the heat.

When the sun ducked far enough behind the buildings, Maggie muttered to herself, "I think it's cool enough ta go to a dumpster agin. It's gonna be Grocery Outlet this time. Hope there's somethin good there."

She found a bag of clothes beside the door behind Goodwill and picked them up. It contained a pair of khaki colored pants along with a pink short sleeved blouse. She changed into her new outfit in the rest room at McDonalds. The pants were a little large at the waist, but the blouse was long enough to cover them up. Changing into the new clothes made her feel better now that she no longer wore the dirty ones.

When she reached the dumpster, the grateful grey haired woman pulled her cart up next to the large blue container. She took the wooden box she salvaged from her last dumpster delving sojourn out of her cart and placed it next to the dumpster. Maggie opened the lid, stepped up on the box and peeked into what she considered to be the table for her next meal.

Suddenly, she let out a piercing high pitched scream and dropped the lid with a resounding bang that reverberated up and down the alley.

Maggie jumped off the box. "Help, somebody help me!" Two people who happened to be in the alley at the same time as Maggie heard her cries and came running.

The first Good Samaritan was one of the employees of the Grocery Outlet store. Dressed in jeans, short sleeved shirt and a long white apron, he ran over to Maggie, who now cried, with huge sobs emanating from her mouth.

"Ma'am, ma'am sit down and tell me what's the matter. Why are you so distraught?"

"There's a dead body in the dumpster," Maggie said, ending with a big, long sniffle. "Call the police!"

The employee, not quite believing what she said, opened the dumpster lid and peeked inside. He immediately dropped it.

"She's right," the employee said to the other Good Samaritan who attempted to calm Maggie down.

The employee took his cell phone out of his pocket and dialed 911. When he hung up he said, "They'll be here in a few minutes."

Motioning to the person trying to calm Maggie down, he said, "I'll be right back. I need to tell my manager what's happening."

"Okay."

In a few minutes, the employee came back with the manager. The manager also lifted the lid and took a look inside the dumpster.

"Wow! Looks like somebody did a job on this guy." He gestured to the employee, "Keep people from coming back here."

A few minutes later, several police cars arrived. David Amhurst and Carlos Lopez cordoned off the area with crime scene tape.

The third cop to arrive on the scene took one look at Maggie and said, "Oh my God, it's the same woman that found the two parts of that guy someone murdered. She's gotta have a connection somehow."

"I don't know, they said she passed a polygraph," said David. "She must be innocent."

"Really? Maybe this time they'll find out she's guilty after all. Some people who are guilty can pass polygraphs."

"Yeah, maybe they will."

Lee and Cat arrived soon after the police put up the crime scene tape. Lee said, "Okay, let's get him out of the dumpster so we can take a look."

His first words after looking at the body were, "Well, looks like we found Manny Sawyer."

While they waited for the Medical examiner to arrive, Cat said, "Shall we go into the dumpster to see if we can find any evidence?"

Lee replied, "No thanks, not this time. Once is enough for me. Let's let the cops do it."

Carlos Lopez was assigned to the job. He only looked in the dumpster a few seconds when he said, "Holy shit! I think I found another piece of that other guy that was murdered and chopped up."

He came up holding a leg.

Cat responded with, "Yeah, it looks like it to me."

Right after they lifted the leg out of the dumpster, the Medical Examiner arrived. "Hey, Hey! We gotta stop meeting like this," Edward said with a big grin on his face.

"You're right about that," Cat said. "We've got a lot for you this time. I'd *say* one and a half victims, but there's really not half of a victim here.

Edward remarked with a smirk, "Looks like you've got a *leg up on 'em* this time guys.
"How do you come up with stuff like this all the time Ed?" Cat lightly poked him on the shoulder with her fist.

"Been around you guys too long I guess."

When Edward finished his exam, he said, "Looks like somebody stabbed this guy several times. I'll let you know what I think he was stabbed with after I get him to the morgue. This body part probably *is* from your other murder victim. Will let you know as soon as I can."

"Thanks Ed, we'll see you later," Lee said.

"Okee Dokee, tah, tah."

Next Lee and Cat turned their attention to Maggie who the police detained for questioning. She seemed more calm.

Cat said, "We don't think you are guilty of killing these men. However, it is very strange that you are the one who is finding them in the dumpsters."

Lee added, "The killer must somehow know which dumpster you are going to next. Do you have any idea how he might know that?"

"Yes, I think I do. The night before I go dumpster diving, I put my cart out near the dumpster I'm going to get into the next day."

Lee slapped his forehead. "And each night he goes around to your favorite ones until he finds the one where your cart is."

"Yes, I think that is how he knows which dumpster I will be going to."

"But how does he know it's *your* cart?" Cat asked. "There are lots of carts left outside near dumpsters."

"I have a metal plate I attached to the side of my cart. AIN'T HOMELESS. I BELONG TO MAGGIE McGRAW

Chapter 15

Lee and Cat, feeling positive the killer knew which dumpster Maggie would be at each time, prepared to set a trap. They decided to stake out an alley. The plan required Maggie to take her cart to a dumpster site. A place with the least chance for the killer to escape.

Lee and Cat would be in an area overlooking the alley. Since they wanted to catch the killer red handed, as soon as he or she dumped the next body part, they planned to rush in and make an arrest. However, if by some chance the killer escaped, A SWAT team waiting a short distance away could go into action.

This seemed like the best way to catch whoever slaughtered Ron Wolford and possibly murdered Manny Sawyer.

While the detectives made their plans, the killer considered what the next move should be. The freezer lid opened disclosing the depths of the unnatural grave of Ron Wolford. Since there hadn't been any advanced planning, a problem arose that needed to be solved. *All these body parts are too large, too heavy or too awkward to lug to a dumpster.*

The time seemed right for other actions. Discarding the parts separately, there was a chance of getting caught. Therefore, it became clear what needed to be done.

Somehow, every part left of the body would have to be taken to the dumpster at the same time. Every part was already packaged. The only thing left to do was to load the packages into the little red wagon he bought the day before.

The killer had located Maggie's cart. It was already at one of the dumpsters. Easy as pie. So predictable!

Pacing back and forth, time passed slowly. Hands on the clock seemed to never move.

Still pacing, an abundance of thoughts came to mind. *I have to be careful. Manny caught me. I wonder if anyone else knows I killed Ron? I have to make sure there's no one there waiting for me before I toss the rest of the body in the dumpster.*

The clock struck on the hour. It was time. A black-gloved hand opened the freezer. The wagon waited next to the freezer. Pulling it closer until it touched the side of the freezer, the packages were tossed into it. The heavy load in the wagon made it difficult to get it into the trunk of the car. Finally, the lid of the trunk closed.

You're on your way to the final resting place you deserve. You son of a bitch!

The drive to the dumpster was uneasy with a trunk-load of human remains. What waited at the dumpster?

If Manny knew why I killed Ron, how many other people knew it too? I wonder how he found out? I'll finish this and deal with it later.

The killer drove into the dumpster area and switched the lights off. The car sat far enough away to make sure no one could spot it. While waiting for the garbage truck, the area was continuously scanned for any sign of anyone else in the area.

Lee and Cat waited at such a distance that the killer could not see them. However, close enough to use binoculars to view the dumpster.

It seemed like such a long time before the garbage truck arrived. Eventually it made its appearance. Everyone watched as the truck emptied the dumpster. The murderer's hands began to sweat. Time passed for a long time after the truck disappeared. Finally, deciding no one else was in the area, the driver pulled the car up to the dumpster.

Lee watched the dumpster through his binoculars then sat up straight. "Cat, someone just drove up to the dumpster and parked."

Cat raised her binoculars. "I see him. As soon as the driver throws something into the dumpster, we'll go in."

Lee called the SWAT team. Just in case he escaped, they should be ready to go.

They watched the killer open his trunk.

"Isn't that Joseph Carlson?" Cat exclaimed.

"Yes!" Holy shit! I wouldn't have guessed he was the killer."

Joseph hauled the wagon out of the trunk and rolled it up to the dumpster. He threw half the contents into the dumpster.

Lee started the car. "Let's go in!" Racing to the dumpster, he screeched to a halt and they jumped out with guns drawn.

Cat shouted, "You're under arrest Joseph! Put your hands up."

Joseph dumped the rest of the wagon's contents. He swiveled and threw the wagon at Lee and Cat. It hit them both. It offered him enough time to run towards his car.

Cat lifted her gun and shot. The bullet hit Joseph in the arm as he closed his car door. The detectives struggled to recover from the wagon blow. He floored the gas pedal and headed straight for them. They both jumped out of the way as he passed them.

Cat was too slow. The mirror hit her in the arm. It spun her around and knocked her to the ground again.

Lee grabbed his cell phone and contacted the SWAT team. "Move in now! He's getting away! He's in that white car." He immediately attended to Cat's arm.

The SWAT team moved in. Three men lifted rifles to stop Joseph before he escaped. One of the SWAT team members held a megaphone, "Stop! Give up now!"

He stomped on the gas pedal even harder and sped past them. They opened fire, hitting the car on all sides. Windows shattered. Glass flew everywhere. The car hit the curb and jumped over it. It smashed into a curbside post office mailbox.

The SWAT team rushed in. They pulled Joseph from the car as Lee and Cat arrived.

Lee, aware that Joseph was dying from several gunshot wounds rushed forward. "Why did you kill Ron?" he asked.

Blood oozed from Joseph's mouth and his ears. "He had an affair with my wife," he replied in a barely audible voice. "They cheated on me."

"Why did you kill Manny?"

"Somehow he knew I killed Ron."

Blood spurted from Joseph's mouth.   He closed his eyes. Lee felt for a pulse.

None

Chapter 16

Cat would have liked to take a couple days off to recuperate from the collision with the mirror on Joseph's car. However, they wanted to tie up the last parts of their case. First, they took a break to discuss what they needed to do. The first thing on the agenda was to let Katrina know they caught the killer.

"You know, there's one thing that I keep wondering about," said Lee. "Where did Joseph kill and cut up Ron's body? It's really bugging me."

"I've been thinking the same thing. He certainly couldn't have done it at the apartment complex. There must be some other place private enough that no one else would have access to it."

"When we let Katrina know we caught Ron's killer, let's find out if she knows whether Joseph owned or rented any place he could have used."

They drove to Katrina's apartment complex. Both were pleased to break the news to Ron's wife. They arrived at Katrina's apartment and knocked on the door. She looked as if she had been doing a lot of grieving for her husband when she answered.

"We have some good news for you," said Cat. "We caught the man who killed your husband."

"Oh thank heaven. How did you catch him?"

"We figured out how he was deciding which dumpster in which to deposit Ron's body parts. Then we caught him in the process of doing it. The SWAT team was forced to kill him. It turned out to be Joseph Carlson."

"What! Oh, my gosh. I can't believe it was Joseph. Why would he kill Ron?"

Cat threw a quick glance at Lee, then said, "We have

no idea. He didn't say why before he died."

"Do you happen to know of any place that Joseph owned," Lee asked, "or rented where he could have killed and dismembered Ron's body?"

"I don't have any idea where he could have. He never spoke of any such place."

When they left Katrina's apartment, Cat said, "I decided she didn't have to know why he killed Ron. She's suffered enough."

"I agree," Lee replied. "Let's go by Anita Carlson's apartment and see if she knows of any place Joseph had. Somewhere perfect enough to kill and dismember a person."

Anita answered the door with tears in her eyes. She had already been notified that it was Joseph who killed Ron. She also knew the police killed him. Lee rolled his eyes at Cat.

He spoke sarcastically to Anita, "Crying for Joseph or for Ron? We know you had an affair with Ron."

"Don't judge me. You don't know the reasons why I had an affair with Ron."

"In the first place, we aren't in the business of judging people," said Cat. "In the second place, did it have to be with someone who just had a baby?"

"He was the one who came on to me. He was in need of something she couldn't give him at the time and I had my own reasons why I needed someone to love me."

"Anyway, we need to ask you something," said Lee. "Did you and Joseph own or rent a place where he could have killed and dismembered Ron?"

Anita thought for a moment and then answered, "Yes, come to think of it, he bought an old garage across town a long time ago where he kept an extra car we had at the time because there was only room for one car here at the apartments. The house had burnt down and the owners never rebuilt it, so they sold the garage to Ron.

We haven't had that car in years. Let me see if I can find a key. I think we had an extra one."

She disappeared and about fifteen minutes later returned with two keys. "One of these should fit the lock on the garage door."

"Okay, let's go," said Cat.

Anita grabbed her coat, locked the door and accompanied them to the car.

Lee, Cat and Anita sped off in a flash. Anita guided them to the property where a garage sat by itself on a good sized lot.

Lee turned to Anita as they left the car. "Let me have the keys. Stay in the car. No telling what we're going to find in there."

The detectives cautiously approached the garage with guns drawn. Cat knocked on the door. No one opened it. Lee tried one of the keys. It didn't work. He tried the other one. It clicked.

Lee entered the dark room. Cat followed closely behind him, searching the wall for a light switch. It clicked as the lights illuminated the room.

Cat's mouth dropped open. "Oh my God, Lee!"

Blood was everywhere in the room. It was unmistakable on two work benches. Drops splattered on one wall. Huge pools collected on the floor. Most of it was dried, except for puddles on the floor. Blood covered a chainsaw hanging on the wall.

Lee examined it. "This must be what he used to dismember Ron's body."

A freezer occupied a corner of the garage. Lee opened it. There was nothing inside but a few spots of blood captured in the freezer frost.

"He must have kept the cut up body parts in here," said Cat. "How gruesome!"

"We need to have CSI come here," said Lee, "and take pictures and see if they can pick up Ron's and Joseph's fingerprints."

"Plus check for any other evidence so we can close this case," Cat added.

Cat put in a call for crime scene investigators to come and do their job. They waited in the car with Anita.

"This is the place where the bodies were cut up," Lee told Anita.

Anita cried as she said, "I can't believe Joseph could have done something like this. It wasn't like him. He had such an even temperament."

Cat replied, "Maybe you're lucky we caught him before he decided to do the same thing to you."

CSI arrived before they could discuss it further. They took over, signifying the final phase of Lee and Cat's investigation.

Chapter 17

The sight of all that gore plus the pain she still felt from being hit by the mirror left Cat a little under the weather. The morning after finding the bloody place where Joseph butchered Ron's body, Lee called her. Since she seemed more than a little upset, it gave him a reason to contact her.

"I just wanted to find out how you're doing today."

"I've felt better. Maybe the way the case ended plus the pain in my arm has me a little down today."

"Why don't you come over to my apartment? I'll fix us some breakfast. Maybe we can watch a little TV afterward. I'll see if I have something that might help the bruise on your arm too."

"Okay, thanks Lee. I'll be right over."

Cat and Lee only lived a few minutes from each other. While she drove there she thought about him. *Lee's a good guy. Plus he isn't bad to look at. I've always had a hankering to get to know him better. I know he doesn't have a wife, but I don't think he has a girlfriend either. I've never heard him talk about one. I think it would be interesting to see what he's like when we aren't working a case. I wonder if he's a good kisser?*

While waiting for Cat to arrive, Lee experienced a sense of excitement. He definitely wanted a closer relationship to Cat than simply a working one. It would even be nice if they became a couple someday. He was a little rusty at dating. It had been a while since he'd been on a date. He figured it was like riding a bicycle. It wouldn't take long to remember how to do it.

His insecurities melted away as soon as he caught sight of Cat standing in his doorway. A ray of sunshine coming through a hallway window fell on her brown hair. It gave the lighter strands an illusion of gold streaks. It continued down her body ending at her breasts, highlighting the low cut top she wore. Lee quickly raised his gaze to her face.

"Hi, come in and have a seat and make yourself comfortable. I was already fixing my breakfast when I talked to you, so yours will be ready in a few minutes too. Would you like some coffee while you wait?"

"Sure, I love coffee and I need a little something to start today off. Yesterday was a little unsettling. That was quite a finish we had to a really ghastly case.

He brought her a large cup of coffee. "Here you go."

She grasped it with one hand and took a drink. "Mmmm," she murmered, closing her eyes. "That tastes really good." Her other hand clutched the bottom of the cup. Flinching, she cried out with a short "Ahh!"

Lee, about to dish up what he cooked, looked and noticed Cat clutching her arm. He immediately turned and went over to her.

"Are you sure you don't need to see your doctor about that? It could be infected."

"No. I'm fine. It's just really sore. It'll be okay in a few days."

"Maybe I have something in my bathroom that might make it feel better. Let me take a look at it.

"Okay," Cat said as she slid her arm from the sleeve of her blouse.

Standing in front of Cat, Lee raised the sleeve to look at her arm. He slid his other hand softly up the back of her arm. She could smell his aftershave. It smelled so good she felt like sniffing it. But she suppressed the tendency and continued to enjoy the scent without making him aware of it.

Lee noticed a large purplish looking bruise on her arm. "Oh Cat, that doesn't look very good. Sit down.

I'm going to see if I have something to put on it." He went into the bathroom and opened the cabinet door. He came out of the bathroom with something to put on Cat's bruise. She stood and was calm as he lifted the sleeve on her blouse and spread it gently on her arm.

"What is that stuff?"

"I don't know. My doctor gave it to me when I had a bruise on my leg."

Lee let go of her sleeve and lightly stroked the back of her bruised arm with his right hand. He put his left hand behind her other shoulder and pulled her to him. Her full breasts leaned against his chest. His lips came close to hers. Without warning, impetuously, he kissed her. She surprised him when she wrapped her arms around him and returned his kiss.

Cat whispered, "I thought you'd *never* get around to doing that."

Suddenly passion dominated the scene. Cat reached over, grabbed the sleeve that was already off her arm and slipped the rest of the blouse over her head. Her kisses became more intense and sensual.

Lee caressed Cat's back then managed to undo the hooks to her bra. She quickly removed it and tossed it aside. He removed the top he wore and with one arm hurled it practically clear across the room. They resumed hugging and kissing.

Lee suddenly stopped and still holding her close, whispered in her ear. "I don't know if we should be doing this, but right now, I don't care."

Cat held him closer and replied, "Me neither." Then she started kissing him again.

Lee suddenly picked her up and carried her into the bedroom. He removed her slacks. She was not wearing panties. Removing the rest of his clothes, he gently laid her down on the bed.

After having sex, they laid in each other's arms. The stress induced by their murder case finally seemed far behind them. There was no talk of the future. They simply enjoyed each other's company and the pleasure of being partners.

Cat pondered, "I wonder what our next case is going to be like?"

Lee responded, "I don't know, but I hope it's not going to be as wild as this one was.

Somehow, they had forgotten breakfast. It was now getting quite cold in the kitchen.

Chapter 18

Residents of the apartment building believed harm no longer threatened their safety. The police caught and killed the person who killed and butchered them. They didn't have any idea how wrong they would soon be. Another killer with the same characteristics as Joseph Carlson lurked close by.

Two short weeks after the police killed Joseph, Christopher Lockhart woke up to find his hands tied above his head. He attempted to move his legs and became aware that someone had tied his feet to a metal ring protruding from the floor.

Raising his head, he saw a familiar figure standing in front of him. "Why are you doing this?"

The person gazing at him replied, "I'll tell you why you're here. However, it won't make any difference. The outcome is going to be the same. You could beg me to spare your life and I'm still going to kill you."

"Oh God, please don't kill me." An agonized look suddenly became stamped on his face. "I'll do whatever you want. Do you want money? You can have however much you want. Just tell me what you want. I'll do or give you whatever you want." The man was clearly terrified.

His begging went unheeded.

"How did I get here? I don't remember anything."

"You shouldn't have been so quick to have a drink with someone. I put something in your drink. It was easy to push you into the back seat of my car. You slept like a baby by the time I started it."

"Whatever I've done, give me a chance to make it right."

"Too late!" the abductor said. "You'll not live to see dawn break on another day."

Unexpectedly, before Christopher spoke another word, the kidnapper picked up a knife.

"No! Don't! Please, please. I'll do anything."

The person wielding the knife laughed. Then, whispering in Christopher's ear said, "Do you think your pitiful requests are going to change anything?"

Swiftly, without another word spoken, the knife rose high. Christopher twisted as it came at him. It pierced his flesh.

He bellowed! "Ahhh!"

The pain was horrible. The urge to throw up hit him. However, he managed to curb the impulse.

He had been *intentionally* stabbed without too much depth. The knife slowly retracted from Christopher's flesh. "This is just the beginning."

"Oh my God, please, please don't hurt me anymore. I'll do anything to make up for *whatever* I've done."

"Sorry. You can beg all you want. Today you will die. But first you're going to hurt more than you've ever hurt before."

Another stab! This time, on his side. Also not deep. It brought a cry of agony to his lips. A piercing scream rang out. Tears streamed down his face.

"Please, if you're going to kill me, make it quick."

Instead, a slice down his chest brought about another ear piercing scream. "I hope God punishes you for this," he bellowed. He twisted in the ropes binding his hands and feet.

His captor raised the knife and thrust it deep into Christopher's chest. A look of horror and disbelief came over his face. His head dropped and he died.

The killer backed up and literally fell into a chair, completely spent. It took half an hour to regain enough energy to think what the next move should be. The plan simply needed to be executed, every detail to be followed.

Rising from the chair, the killer cut the rope holding Christopher's hands and feet. It took every ounce of strength to place the body on a high bench. Every inch of the murderer's clothing was covered with plastic outer wear. The killer put on a welder's mask. Then, started a chainsaw and made the first cut.

Blood spurted everywhere in the room. It was on the bench, the floor and the chainsaw. Several large drops splattered on the wall. The killer was covered in blood.

When the body was dissected, each piece was transferred to plastic wrap that had been laid out on a different bench.

Each wrapped body part was moved to a freezer standing in a corner. Then the killer shed the blood drenched paraphernalia and dumped them into a large waste basket. The only thing left to do was discard one of the body parts in a place already selected.

The killer looked over the body parts to choose which one to dispose of first.

"You deserve this as much as Ron and Joseph."

Chapter 19

Victor Paulson called Katrina Wolford. "Katrina, it's Vic. I think we should all get together. We need to talk about what happened to Ron and Manny. Will you call Hazel and Anita and set up a time and place?"

"Yes, of course. I've been wanting to talk to you guys anyway. There's some questions *I* have about what happened too."

When Katrina called Anita, she asked, "Why does Vic want a meeting with us?"

"I don't know. He just said he thought we should all get together," Katrina answered. *Wow! She sounds defensive.*

Hazel, however, appeared to be really interested in the meeting. "I think we *should* have one too. There are a lot of things left unanswered as far as I'm concerned."

The meeting, set up the next day, started as soon as Victor came home from work. Katrina, Hazel and Anita showed up early and waited nervously for him. When he arrived, he noticed Katrina and Hazel on one end of the huge tan circular sofa and Angela on the other end. Anita rested in the large, soft padded chair that matched the sofa. Angela supplied each of them with coffee.

Once Angela gave Victor a cup of coffee, he began the meeting. "I thought we should get together because I think there are a lot of issues to discuss, in my mind at least, concerning Ron's murder and Joseph's death. I have a lot of questions that haven't been answered."

"Me too," responded Hazel.

"I disagree," Anita said. "I think we should forget it and move on."

Victor raised his hand. "Some of us know why you disagree Anita."

75

"What do you mean by that?" Hazel asked.

"I think you should tell us what you mean by that, Vic," Angela said with sarcasm in her voice.

Victor replied, "No, why don't *you* tell us what I mean by that, Anita?"

Katrina, who had been listening intently, asked, "What's going on here?"

Anita stood up and answered sharply, "He means, you stupid idiot, that Joseph killed your husband because he was having an affair with me. Now you know *what* he meant by that."

Katrina stared at Anita. Tears immediately came to her eyes. She shook her head. "I've been grieving for a no good, two-timing SOB."

"Victor stepped in saying, "Okay! okay! Ladies, settle down. There are still some questions that we should ask ourselves. We know why Joseph killed Ron, but we still don't know why he killed Manny."

Hazel replied, "Maybe *Manny* was also having an affair with you Anita. If he was, he deserved to die too."

Anita put her hands on her hips and said, "Are you kidding? I wouldn't have had an affair with your husband if he was the only man on earth. He was too ugly."

Hazel stood up and stepped towards Anita.

Victor intervened. "Stop it," he shouted, we need to stick together right now instead of going at each other's throats. There's a new development I've just learned about today. There's another resident of the building missing and it's obviously not one of us. His name is Christopher Lockhart. No one has seen or heard from him for two days. No one has called the cops yet, but the news is going around the building. His wife is supposedly going to call them if he doesn't come home soon. In the meantime, there are things that the police haven't told us."

Victor put his hand up and counted on his fingers,

"First, how did they discover Joseph was the killer? Second, how was Ron killed? Third, how was Manny killed? Fourth, do they even know *why* Manny was killed? We can speculate all we want, but I think we need to have the detectives fill us in on the missing information."

The rest agreed that it was in their best interest to stay together.

Victor said, "If there is another killer out there, how do we know he's not going to kill one of us next?"

Chapter 20

Lately, Maggie didn't worry about finding anything in a dumpster. She helped the detectives find out who the killer was and the SWAT team killed him. However, for the past two weeks, whenever she left her cart at any dumpster, she hung around out of sight for a while to see if anyone followed her. In the early mornings she also went back to the dumpster to watch if anyone came after the garbage truck left. Some apprehension still remained.

Peachie, another homeless person who lived in the woods gave her words of encouragement, "Hey Maggs, you did good helpin 'em get that killer. They should'a given you a medal."

"I only did what anybody else would'a done, Peachie. Wouldn't you'da done it too?"

"Nah, I'da been too scared."

Leaving for her next dumpster diving delight, Maggie replied, "Aw Peachie, I don't believe that for a minute."

It was early evening and the weather turned out to be perfect. Even though she had misgivings lately, Maggie went to the dumpster behind Fred Meyer. She could usually find lots of good food there.

When she arrived at the dumpster, she opened it to take a peek. It looked like there might be a pretty good haul. She closed the lid and walked over to the place where she left her cart the night before. Maggie spotted the cart, but as she grabbed the handle, a male employee of Fred Meyer opened the back door and stepped out with a cart full of food.

Maggie pushed her cart by the employee and as she passed him she noticed him throwing a great deal of food into the dumpster. She took the cart around the corner and kept looking every few minutes until the employee dropped the lid of the dumpster and went back into the grocery store.

Checking the area for anyone else, she found it to be free of any other people. Maggie pushed the cart around the corner and placed it next to the dumpster. She looked around and found something to stand on.

Leaning over the edge of the dumpster, she found some good food items immediately. She picked up three packages of hot dogs *We can make a fire and cook these up for all of us,* a package of salami *Yuk, don't like this, but Peachie does,* two bags of onion and sour cream potato chips *I'll keep these,* and two boxes of donuts *Yum, yum, keep these too.*

Her arms full of food, Maggie stepped down from the dumpster to put it into her cart. That's when she noticed it.

There was a package on the shelf under the main part of the cart. Maggie threw the items she picked out of the dumpster into the cart. She bent down and brought out the package from the lower part of the cart.

The package, wrapped in some kind of colored plastic, wasn't heavy. Maggie felt of the contents. Some of what was inside seemed soft and some of it was hard. *Somebody must'a forgot one of their packages. I hope it's somethin I want or need.*

Maggie started unwrapping the plastic. A blob of something fell from the package. It splashed on her shoe. She reached into her pocket and pulled out a tissue. When she wiped it off her shoe, she examined it.

It was blood.

The stunned woman quickly stuffed the package back in the under part of the cart. She stood there for a couple of minutes unable to move. Recollections of what happened before came back to her. She started shaking. *This can't be happenin again The person who killed those two people is dead. This has gotta be a package of meat.*

When she calmed down enough to stop shaking,

Maggie decided to finish unwrapping the package. She reached into the cart, picked the package up and laid it on top of the cart. When she had unwrapped half of it, the rest popped open.

She stepped back, nearly falling, and let out a shriek. Hiding her face in her hands,

She started sobbing.

The package contained a human hand! *Why, why is this happenin to me again?*

Maggie suddenly wrapped the hand in the plastic and left the area as fast as she could push her cart.

She went directly to the woods where she and her friends lived. Peachie saw her coming. She was still sobbing.

"What's the matter Maggs?"

"You won't believe this, but I found another human hand in my cart."

"What? In your *cart* instead of a dumpster?"

"Yeah, what should I do? Somebody must'a put it in there on purpose."

"You gotta call the cops, Maggs."

"I could just dump it."

"No, you gotta do the right thing."

"What if they think I'm the one that did it this time?"

"Just take another lie detector test to prove you didn't. I know you're innocent. I'm your alibi."

Maggie thought for a while, then said, "Okay, will you go with me?"

"Yeah, don't worry, everything's gonna be fine."

Maggie and Peachie went to the Starbucks at the Safeway store and told the same waitress who had called the manager before that she found another human hand.

Chapter 21

When Lee and Cat received the call that someone discovered another body part, they had already met with Katrina, Hazel, Victor, Angela and Anita to discuss the questions they had about Ron, Manny and Joseph.

Now Lee's face showed a look of disbelief. "What the hell is going on? We caught and killed Joseph. We know he killed Ron and Manny, but he's dead. That means we have another killer on our hands. Can you believe that?"

Cat replied, "Yeah, there has to be another killer."

"Could the new killer be one of the swingers?"

"What about Anita. She didn't seem really upset when she found out we killed Joseph, but maybe she wanted a little revenge."

Lee replied, "Maybe Katrina killed Anita to retaliate for her having an affair with her husband."

"Or it could be Hazel that killed Anita to get revenge because Joseph killed Manny."

"Until we find out who is *not* dead, these are just guesses," said Lee. Victor will be home in a few minutes. Let's go find out if *any* of them are dead. The apartment complex is on the way to the crime scene. It will only take a few minutes to see if they are alive."

"Okay, let's do it now."

They started at Katrina's apartment since Victor wasn't due for a few more minutes. She answered the door with a questionable look.

"Hi, what are you guys doing here?

Lee replied, "Another part of a body has been discovered."

"Oh my God. We heard that another resident had

disappeared. Are you sure it isn't part of Ron's body? Maybe you didn't find them all."

"It's not from Ron," Cat said. "Every part of his body was found according to the Medical Examiner."

"You guys caught Joseph, I know you'll catch this killer too."

"I hope we can," Lee said in a wishful voice.

They said goodbye and decided to visit Hazel next. They found a note on her door saying she was at Anita's apartment.

Anita was surprised to see them so soon after they answered the questions they could about Ron, Manny and Joseph.

Lee spoke to Anita and Hazel. "We want you to know that another part of a body has been discovered. There is another killer who cut someone up. Be careful."

Anita and Hazel couldn't believe that a second killer was also dismembering someone.

Horrified, Anita said, "We know there's another resident missing. Could it be him that somebody chopped up?"

"We don't know yet," Cat replied. "We'll keep you informed."

When they left Anita's apartment, Cat said, "Well, that just leaves Angela and Victor."

Lee glanced at his watch. "Victor should be home by now. Let's see if they are both still alive."

Victor answered the door. He told them Angela was in the kitchen cooking dinner. She called out a hello from the back of the apartment.

"We're happy to see that you're okay. We've been told another resident is missing and we hoped it wasn't one of you two."

Victor replied, "I know who it is. His name's Christopher Lockhart. I think his wife was going to call the cops today."

Cat said, "We are on our way to where the body part was discovered. We'll get a DNA test and it will match Christopher Lockhart."

While driving to the crime scene, Steve said to Cat, "You said the DNA *will* match Christopher Lockhart like you knew it would. You should have said *might* match Christopher Lockhart."

Cat looked away for a couple of seconds, then said, "Yeah, I meant *might* match his DNA."

When they arrived behind Fred Meyer, the area was already blocked off by crime scene tape. A crowd of curious onlookers stood hoping to get a glimpse of something interesting.

Maggie, sitting next to her cart on a chair brought out by a store employee, looked extremely distraught.

Cat approached her and put her hand on her shoulder. "Maggie, here you are again. Someone seems to have it in for you. You keep finding parts of bodies. They seem to know your routine."

"How do they know where I'm gonna leave my cart?" Maggie said with tears streaming down her face. "Why are they doin this to me?"

Lee said, "Show us where you found the body part."

"It's right here 'neath my cart," she said, standing and bending over to show them the package.

She started to pick it up when Lee said, "Don't touch it. We need to have the package fingerprinted before you open it.

Maggie quickly withdrew her hands and sat down again. She started crying again. "Is someone gonna kill me too?"

Cat replied, "I doubt that Maggie. I think someone is just using you to make sure the body parts are found and made public."

"Why couldn't they pick someone else?"

"You're easy because of your routine. Maybe you should change how you do it," Lee remarked.

Cat broke in and said, "No, don't change anything right now. It will make it more difficult to catch the killer if they don't have access to you."

"Okay, but I hope you catch him soon. It makes me not want to leave the woods. I wouldn't if I didn't have to eat."

"Sit back and relax a little bit Maggie, we'll have you out of here soon."

Lee motioned for Cat to follow him. When they went far enough for Maggie to be out of hearing range, he asked, "Do you think there's a possibility Maggie could be the killer this time?"

"No, of course not. How and where could a homeless bag lady kill and dismember anyone?"

"Yeah, I guess you're right. I think we should look the crowd over. Killers like to hang around the commotion caused by their kill. Let's see if there's anyone we've seen before at the other crime scenes."

"Good idea, you take half the crowd and I'll take the other half."

Lee and Cat mingled with the crowd for awhile, then stepped out of the taped off area to confer with each other. Last thing they needed was an interloper.

Cat asked, "Did you see anyone you've seen before at the crime scenes?'

"No, did you?"

"No, no one."

When they walked back to talk to Maggie, Edward Danielson, the medical examiner arrived. He took one look at Lee and Cat and with a sparkle in his eyes, said, "How come I'm seeing so much of you guys lately? I mean, I love you, but this is ridiculous."

Cat replied, "We're tired of seeing you too, because we both know what it means if we do."

Edward laughed and asked, "What have you guys dug up for me this time?"

"It's another body part. You told us you received *all* of Ron Wolford's body, so it's gotta be a different victim this time," Lee replied.

"You guys just don't know how to stay away from trouble, do you?"

"I guess not. The package has already been fingerprinted."

Edward took the package from the cart and opened it. "Another hand! How handy. I can tell it's from a different victim because the fingernails aren't like the ones on the last victim."

"We think we might know who this victim is, so get us the DNA results ASAP. We will have DNA from who we think it is by that time."

"Alright guys, I'll get the DNA result to you as soon as I get it. Stay out of trouble if you can."

"That's not always easy for us."

When Edward left, Lee and Cat turned their attention to Maggie.

Cat asked, "Did you see anyone in or around your cart, Maggie?"

"No, I didn't see no one anywhere behind the stores."

"Okay, the cart's been fingerprinted, so you can take it with you."

Lee added, "Keep up your routine. We may be able to catch the killer in the process of getting rid of another body part. We are going to stake out your next dumpster dive. Are you okay with that?"

"Good, 'cause it scares me just 'ta think about it.

Chapter 22

Maggie wasn't due to put her cart out at one of her favorite dumpsters yet. Most of the dumpster divers she knew carried on their craft just before or after dark.

Lee and Cat decided to do a couple of stakeouts.

Lee chose the dumpster behind Fred Meyer. It gave him a good view of the dumpster without anyone spotting him. He was on his own while Cat staked out a dumpster behind Albertsons.

He stopped at a Taco Time and picked up two burritos and pop for dinner. He drove to the site he picked and settled in for what could be a long night.

It was about an hour after dark when Lee noticed a dark figure approach the dumpster. He lifted his binoculars. It was difficult to tell if the person about to open the dumpster was male or female.

He watched as the figure placed a box next to the dumpster, stepped onto it and opened the lid. The person bent over the edge and placed both arms in the metal container.

Dropping the binoculars, Lee started the engine. He gunned it. As he came upon the dumpster, he turned his flashers on. Jumping out of the car, he pulled his gun and shouted, "Get out of the dumpster and put your hands up."

"Don't shoot! My hands are up."

"Keep your hands up and turn around."

The compliant individual slowly turned around while trying not to fall off the box. Lee scrutinized a tall skinny man dressed in baggy grey pants who stared back at him with wide open eyes. A short grey beard and shoulder length grey hair framed brown eyes dimmed from age.

"I didn't know it was against the law to look for food in a dumpster. Honest! Please don't arrest me."

"Get off the box slowly and move to the side of the dumpster. Keep your hands up."

The man carried out Lee's orders. Lee walked to the other side of the dumpster with the gun still trained on the elderly man.

"What did you put in the dumpster?"

"Nothing, I was looking for food. I haven't eaten all day. Let me go, please."

Lee glanced into the dumpster and poked around for a couple of minutes. Seeing no package that looked like the first one Maggie found, Lee said, "You can put your hands down now. You're not under arrest, but go find another dumpster somewhere else."

The man picked up a bag lying next to him and turned to leave.

Lee asked, "What's in the bag?"

"Half of a sandwich I found in another dumpster. It wasn't enough to eat so I thought I'd try this one to see if I could find something to go with it."

Lee walked over to the scraggly looking man. "Let me take a look at it."

The distressed man held the bag out. Lee took it and checked the contents. It contained half of a sandwich.

Handing the bag back to the man Lee said, "Okay, now get out of here before I *do* arrest you."

"Yes sir!" The grateful homeless man scurried off as quickly as he could.

Lee, disappointed that he hadn't caught the killer, went back to his car. He drove back to the place he could watch the dumpster from without being seen. The night wasn't over. He might get lucky yet.

He was ready to give up when he noticed a car enter the alley. Lifting his binoculars again, he made out another shadowy figure of the evening. Lee started the car in case he needed to make a speedy exit from his advantage point.

Someone dressed in dark pants was sneaking up to the dumpster. A hooded jacket covered the face of the person sneaking up to the dumpster. Whoever it was held a package in one hand.

Lee threw down the binoculars and floored the accelerator. He turned on his flashers.

The person scrutinizing the area one last time before throwing the package in the dumpster saw him coming. The hooded individual turned and made it halfway to the car when Lee came to a screeching halt in front of the dumpster. Gun in hand, he leaped out of the car.

He yelled, "Stop, put your hands up!"

The suspect kept running.

Running after the defiant person, Lee shouted again, "Stop or I'll shoot!"

The fleeing suspect ignored his warning, determined to get away. Getting close to the car, Lee shot over their heads. The person evading arrest kept running. He sent a second shot closer to the suspect. Somehow, the person in question made it to the car. Right when Lee arrived to his car, the escaping suspect drove off at an accelerated rate of speed.

Lee shot the back window out and then attempted to shoot out one of the tires. Unsuccessful, he scrambled to his car. The suspect's car rounded the corner of the strip mall by the time he started the chase. When he turned the corner, the car was no longer in sight.

"Shit! Where did you go?" he muttered.

He had come out beside a theater. The parking lot was still full of cars since most of the movies had not let out yet. On a hunch, he drove slowly up and down rows of parked cars in the lot. He passed behind about half of the cars in the lot when one pulled out and took off fast enough to squeal the tires.

"Gotcha!" Lee exclaimed.

Lee pursued the car out of the parking lot onto a short street. It passed a gas station out to a traffic light. Lights flashing, Lee sped after the fleeing suspect. The stoplight turned red. The possible killer never even slowed down.

The escaping car turned an abrupt right. Lee, taking a chance, started to turn right also. An oncoming car halfway through the light, hit the left back fender of Lee's car. It spun him almost completely around. Lee watched the car with a missing rear view window as it vanished into the distance.

Lee called for assistance for both the accident and the dumpster which was now a crime scene. Officer Buzz Wilcox arrived a few minutes later. Lee gave him information he needed.

Lee also said, "I'll be at the crime scene at the dumpster behind Fred Meyer.

He tried to call Cat, but she didn't answer her cell phone. *She's probably sound asleep at her stakeout.* He could tell her about his night in the morning.

When he was about to leave the crime scene, he realized he no longer had a car. He walked to the accident. When he arrived at the scene of the accident, he discovered his car had already been hauled away. He stopped and thanked Officer Buzz Wilcox. The officer gave him a ride home.

He was close to home when Cat called. "I must have turned my phone off and when I noticed it, I saw that you tried to call me."

"How did *your* dumpster watch go?" Lee asked.

"Really uneventful. Didn't see anyone all night long. How did yours go?"

"I think I almost caught our killer, but they got away. I'll tell you all about it tomorrow."

It was late when Lee arrived home. Way past his bed time. He went right to bed. However, he couldn't go to sleep. He kept thinking about the one that got away.

Chapter 23

When Lee woke up the next morning, he called Cat. "Let's meet for breakfast and I'll tell you about my encounter with the killer. We need to talk."

"Okay, I'm anxious to hear about it."

Lee rushed to meet Cat, eager to recount the happenings of the previous evening. He arrived at the restaurant twenty minutes before Cat.

Cat finally arrived. Lee commenced telling her the details of his confrontation with the killer as soon as they ordered breakfast.

"I thought sure I had him, but he escaped at the dumpster. However, I shot his back window out."

"I take it he got away."

"Yeah, he did. He thought he was clever, but I spotted him in the parking lot of the theater."

Cat, very attentive, asked, "Then what happened?"

"As soon as I saw him, he sped off. I almost caught him again at the light, but that's when the son of a bitch made a real quick right turn as the light was turning red. I tried to follow him, but some guy hit me as I was turning. The bastard got away."

"We need to have all the cops looking for someone with a missing back window," Cat said,

"Definitely, good thing I have a back up car at home. It's an old jalopy, but it still runs. Now we should talk to the swingers. We have the DNA results from the dumpster body part. They should know the results."

"I agree. Let's ask Victor to get them all together."

Lee called Victor to assemble the rest of the swingers. He told him the DNA test results on the body part found in the dumpster had come in.

While they drove to the apartment, Lee was still in an angry mood about letting the killer escape.

"Somehow, we're going to catch that ass hole yet," Lee said with fury in his voice.

"Calm down Lee, we'll get him. Right now let's concentrate on talking to the swingers."

He had cooled off by the time they arrived.

Katrina, Hazel, and Anita gathered in Victor and Angela's apartment.

Lee began the groups meeting by telling them, "We thought you should all know we received some DNA results yesterday. It confirmed the body part discovered in a dumpster is a portion of the body of Christopher Lockhart."

Angela's expression changed. She looked terrified. "It looks like someone is targeting the residents of our apartment complex."

Kristina became panicky, "But *he* wasn't a member of our group, so why was he killed?"

"And besides, Joseph killed Ron and Manny and he's dead," Hazel added.

Cat entered the conversation, "That's right. Therefore, we know there is another killer. We wanted you to know so you would be careful. Christopher Lockhart wasn't part of your group, but that doesn't mean you shouldn't keep a close eye out for each other. Any one of you could be next. However, it doesn't mean that the apartment complex is being targeted. There might not be any more killings. Someone might have had a reason to kill him and it has nothing to do with other residents."

"Right now, we have Christopher's murder to solve," said Lee. Do any of you know Christopher Lockhart?"

"We all knew him," Anita replied. "He came to all of the parties the apartment owners threw."

Victor said, "He seemed like a nice guy, but he was aloof whenever any of us would try to talk to him. I think somehow he knew we were swingers."

Lee looked around at everyone. "Victor is the only male left of your group, so you aren't swinging anymore are you?"

"Not right now, but we *had* a few couples at another apartment building interested in joining us," Victor replied. "Now, I think all the ladies should stick close to home. I have to go out because I work, but I am going to be extra careful."

"I am scared to death," whimpered Angela. "I am definitely not going out. Victor can bring home anything we need."

Katrina, who had been sitting, stood and announced, "I've got enough food to last me quite a while. I am definitely not going out right now either. I just hope you catch this guy soon."

"We are going to do our best to catch him," Cat responded. Please don't do anything to get yourselves in harm's way."

Anita moved over to comfort Angela. "Don't worry, I don't plan to. I'm not even going to answer the door,"

Hazel chimed in, "Me too!"

"We don't know if this killer targeted only Christopher Lockhart or has plans to kill other people," Lee said. "So until we catch him, please, just be careful."

Once Lee and Cat believed the swinger group would do what they should to stay safe, they said their goodbyes.

When they drove away, they started talking about what their next move might be. During their conversation, Lee said, "I don't understand how these guys can do what they do. I couldn't trade off my wife or husband to *anyone*."

"Don't knock it," Cat replied, "until you've tried it."

Chapter 24

Maggie wanted to stop leaving her cart at the dumpster she selected to dive in. Cat told her, "Don't change your routine right now. It might make catching the killer easier."

The next time Maggie planned to take her cart to one of her favorite dumpsters, she and Peachie sat in the woods talking to each other. Maggie was still quite upset over finding the first body part from the second killer.

Peachie asked, "Do ya know which dumpster yer gonna put yer cart at next Maggs?"

"Dunno yet. I'm scared ta death to put it anywhere, but Lee and Cat want me ta keep on doin what I've been doin. I know if I find another body part, I'm not gonna touch it this time. It gives me the creeps. I think I'd recognize the package if I saw one."

"Why don't we go get somethin for lunch and dinner now Maggs. If ya want me to, I'll go with ya tonight ta put yer cart out."

"Okay Peachie. I'm hungry already. Let's go."

The two frumpy bag ladies ambled out of the woods to one of their preferred restaurant dumpsters. When they reached their destination, Peachie ran on ahead of Maggie.

"Come on Maggs!" Peachie yelled. "There's gotta be somethin good in here."

Maggie stopped near the dumpster. Then she backed away. She could feel anxiety nearly overtake her. Close to having a panic attack, she said, "Ya go ahead Peachie. I'm scared of what I might find in there."

"Okay Maggs. I'll see if I can scrounge enough for both of us."

Peachie found something to stand on and rummaged around in the dumpster for about fifteen minutes. She handed Maggie the results of her quest. Maggie deposited them in her cart.

When Peachie finished sorting through the dumpster, Maggie asked, "Ya didn't find any package like the ones I've been findin?"

"No, nothin like that. Stop bein a worry wart. Yer not gonna find any more of them packages."

"I'm still scared I'm gonna find another one."

"Let's get these things sorted and have some lunch."

Peachie and Maggie made their way back to the woods and divided what Peachie found. Lunch and dinner came and went. That night, Maggie and Peachie decided which dumpster to put the cart next to. They trudged off with the cart and left it at the site they chose.

Maggie said, "I hope Lee and Cat can catch the killer tonight. I did my part."

The next morning, Maggie awoke later than usual because she was feeling exhausted. The anxiety over what she found in some dumpsters made her that way. No matter how much she attempted to dispel those feelings, the terror petrified her.

It was already late. If Lee and Cat caught anyone the night before, she should have heard by now.

Peachie tried to calm Maggie. "Do ya want me ta go with ya when ya go to the dumpster today?"

"No," Maggie replied, "I'm a big girl. I can do this alone. I just need ta tell myself I'm not going ta find any body parts and believe it."

It was late afternoon when she summoned enough courage to go to the dumpster where she had parked her grocery cart.

By now there should be plenty of good stuff in the dumpster.

The first thing Maggie decided to do was look in her

cart and check for a package. She looked on the top and
bottom of the cart and let out a sigh of relief when there
was nothing there. Gaining a little more confidence,
she moved her cart next to the dumpster and found
something to stand on. Taking in a huge breath, Maggie
opened the dumpster.

There's a lot of good stuff here.

She explored the top layer of the dumpster's contents.
Placing a loaf of bread, a jar of peanut butter and a bag
of potato chips into her cart, Maggie returned to the
goodies inside the dumpster.

While lifting a magazine from the top of several
items, she saw it.

A package wrapped in the same paper as the one she
previously discovered lay in her sight.

The agony Maggie suffered before returned like a
smack in the face. She shook her head in disbelief. She
wanted to cry, but was too shocked to bring any tears to
her eyes. Looking around, she realized there was no one
to ask for help.

Maggie ran around the building looking for anyone
that could help her. There was a man ready to enter his
car. She ran up to him and grabbed the door before he
could close it.

"Please help me. I need ta call the police and I don't
have a cell phone. Could ya call them for me?"

"Why do you want to call the police? Are you okay?"
Are you in danger?"

"No, I found part of a body in the dumpster here. If
ya call them, I'll talk ta them."

The man made a call to the police department and
turned the phone over to Maggie. She started to cry.
When she finished talking to the dispatcher, the man said
to Maggie,"Sit in my car until the police arrive."

"Thank ya, I'm so upset I need a place ta sit down."

"Did I hear you right when you said you found a part of a body?"

"Yes, I found part of a body in the dumpster."

"Oh, my goodness! That's awful."

"It's not the first time. They're sendin the detectives I know too. I can't believe it happened agin."

Chapter 25

Lee called Cat to have her meet him at the scene. He notified her what Maggie found in the dumpster

She answered his call sounding weak. "I'm too sick Lee. You'll have to investigate this time without me."

"Okay, I'll call you when I'm finished and let you know if there are any new developments."

Aware that Cat had been ill for several days, he hoped she was better. Unfortunately it wasn't the case.

When he arrived at the crime scene, Maggie still sat in the back seat of the man's car. Lee introduced himself. Then he opened the car door and slid in beside Maggie. She appeared to be quite upset yet.

"So you think you found another body part."

"I'm *sure* it's another body part. It has the same kind of wrapping paper as the other one."

"Alright Maggie, let's go over to the dumpster. You can show me the package."

She and Lee ducked under the police tape and went to the dumpster. Maggie opened the lid. She pointed to the package. Lee confirmed the wrapping paper looked the same as the first body part had been wrapped in.

"I think you're right Maggie."

Maggie started to cry. "Why didn't ya stake out the cart like ya said you and Cat would? If ya had, ya probly would'a caught the killer."

"I'm sorry Maggie, we intended to do that, but Cat was sick. We wanted to do the stakeout together. Since she was ill, I helped investigate another case instead. I promise, next time, I'll be there even if Cat isn't. When are you planning to take the cart out again?"

"Since I didn't get much today, I think I'll put it out

again tonight."

"Okay, I'll be there when the trash guy empties the dumpster. In the meantime, why don't you take your cart and get some rest until tonight. I don't need for you to stay here any longer."

"Oh, thank goodness," Maggie said in an ecstatic voice. "I'm so glad I don't have ta stay."

When she left, Lee called the Medical Examiner. Edward's voice changed from a business tone to a cheerful one when he realized who called him.

"I think another body part has been found in a dumpster Ed. I need you to come and confirm it."

"You can't seem to keep your bodies together any more, Lee. Didn't you learn how to do it in your Murder 101 classes?"

"Okay smart ass. Just get your buns over here. I need your professional opinion about whether this is an actual human body part?"

While Lee waited for Edward to arrive, he had one of the cops dust the dumpster and outside of the package for fingerprints. Then he talked with some people milling around outside the crime scene tape to see if anyone saw or heard anything that might help the investigation. They didn't have anything yet that could help catch this killer. It turned out to be a more difficult case to solve than the swinger case had been.

I wish we could get a break in this case.

Lee thought about Cat. He hoped she would be feeling well soon. Her illness must have been coming on for a while because he thought she had been a little distracted lately. She had been such a great partner. He hated to see her sick.

Once Edward arrived, he and Lee opened the package they retrieved from the dumpster. A human foot without the toes lay in front of them.

"Wonder why the killer cut the toes off?"

"What, no smart remark? That's not like you Ed."

"Can't think of anything off the top of my head, Lee. Give me a second and I'm sure I can come up with something."

Lee laughed. "Well, I guess we don't have to wonder if this is part of a human body anymore."

"Nope, don't think it's going to get up and walk away though."

"I knew it. Didn't take you long to think of a comeback."

They re-wrapped the body part and Edward left with it under his arm.

Lee wound up his investigation and, true to his word, made plans to stakeout the dumpster where Maggie was going to leave her cart.

The trash truck came to empty at this particular dumpster every morning around 6:00 A.M. Lee decided to stakeout the dumpster alone since Cat was still under the weather.

He arrived at the site of the dumpster at 5:00 A.M. and checked to make sure Maggie had left her cart there like she said she would. Then he found a place to wait until the trash truck emptied the dumpster.

At 5:48 A.M. the trash truck arrived and emptied the dumpster. When it left, Lee raised his binoculars. At 6:02 A.M. he saw a car pull up about half a block away from the dumpster. He couldn't see it perfectly clear in the dim light, but it looked to him like the rear window was gone.

Sitting up straighter in the car seat, he held the binoculars up to his eyes with both hands. A figure emerged from the car dressed in dark clothes with a hood pulled tight around the neck.

"Okay, you son of a bitch. Round two coming up!"

Chapter 26

Lee harbored a particular hostility towards this butcher since the first encounter. He watched as a familiar figure dressed in dark pants and jacket emerged from the vehicle. Instantly recognizing the dark hood pulled tightly around the killer's head, Lee watched as the shadowy figure removed something from the trunk of the car. Then he saw the suspect look around for several minutes. The hooded person proceeded towards the dumpster when no one seemed to be in the area.

"Gotcha!" Lee muttered in anticipation.

He dropped one hand to reach for his gun, but kept his eyes on the target headed for the dumpster. Lee lowered the binoculars and started the car. Then he took off from his hiding place with a lurch. The car came to a screeching halt as the killer threw a package into the dumpster. Lee jumped out of the car with his gun aimed at the suspect.

"Put your hands up," Lee shouted.

The person in his line of sight began to run and pulled a gun from the jacket pocket.

"You're under arrest!" Lee yelled.

The killer turned and fired a shot at Lee. The bullet missed and whizzed past his head. He started to run to the other side of the car as the killer took another shot. This time, the bullet grazed his left arm. It hurt like hell, but he wasn't about to let the killer get away again.

The killer was close to making it behind the dumpster, but as Lee rounded the car, he squeezed off another shot. He heard a moan and knew he must have hit the suspect. However, the dark figure made it around behind the dumpster.

Lee reached into the still running car and flipped it out of park. He jumped in and moved the car forward as he crouched behind the steering wheel. Lee reached the side of the dumpster and slammed on the brakes. After putting the car in park, he jumped out. While peeking over the hood of the car he noticed the killer about to disappear around the other end of the dumpster.

"Oh no you don't, you son of a bitch. You're not going to get away again." He steadied his hand on the hood of the car. He took a shot. An agonized cry rang out. The fleeing shadowy figure fell.

Lee ran over to the suspect who lay on his side. He kicked the gun away. He checked for a pulse. The suspect was still alive. Lee pulled the hood off the killer's head. He turned the killer over.

"Oh my God!" Lee said, shocked at who he was looking at. "Cat? For Christ's sake, Cat." He quickly put a hand on his forehead and shook his head. "What the hell have you done?"

He took in a deep breath and let it out before asking, "Did *you* kill Christopher Lockhart?"

Cat didn't answer.

Lee called for an ambulance, then went to the dumpster, opened it and retrieved the package Cat had thrown into it. He unwrapped it enough to tell it was part of a body. Then he laid it on the hood of the car.

He went back to attend to Cat. She was regaining consciousness.

"Don't talk right now, you're hurt pretty bad."

While waiting for the aid car, Lee knelt to check Cat's wound. There was an injury to her shoulder and one in the hip area. It didn't look as if either was life threatening.

"Cat, can you hear me? I called the paramedics."

She looked up at him and said, "Yes, Lee. I'm so

sorry. I hope you'll understand. I wish it hadn't been *you* I disappointed. Please forgive me." She started crying.

"Did *you* kill Christopher Lockhart?"

"Yes, I killed him because one of the swingers told me he threatened them."

"Why? You vowed to uphold the law, not break it."

"I was a swinger myself once, Lee."

"What!" Lee said, appalled.

"I finally got my act together and had been leading a good life until this case came along. I guess I lost it when I learned he threatened the swingers."

"Why didn't you stop throwing the body parts in the dumpsters after I almost nailed you the last time?"

"Just thought I was invincible, I guess."

Cat winced from the pain. Lee comforted her until the paramedics arrived.

Cops arrived soon after that to take care of the crime scene.

When the paramedics lifted the gurney to load Cat into the aid car, she said to Lee, "I hope your next partner is better than I was."

Lee took her hand. "You were a great partner. Fate just dealt you a bad hand. Where is the rest of Christopher Lockhart's body?"

"It's in my garage." She gave him the address since he had never been to her home.

Lee called a tow company to haul Cat's car away. He didn't recognize it during their first encounter because he had never seen it before.

When Lee was finished with the loose ends at the crime scene, he decided to go to the address Cat had given him. A huge three car garage was attached to a large two story home. Cat's car she drove every time she and Lee had been together was sitting in the driveway.

Lee was amazed when he opened the garage door.

One of the bays apparently housed the car Lee had hauled away from the dumpster. The other two looked like scenes from a horror movie. The middle of the area was set up to tie someone's hands above their head so they would either dangle or their feet would touch the floor. A large bench designed to give someone plenty of work space was to the right of that area. Several small items lying on the bench such as a sharp knife and a corkscrew could have been used to torture a person. Blood was everywhere in the room. A hand saw covered with blood rested on the bench. Blood spattered the walls, and floor around the bench. The bench itself was completely covered in blood.

Lee found the rest of Christopher's body in a freezer.

He called CSI. *They will have a lot to keep them busy here and in the house for awhile.*

While he waited for CSI to arrive, he thought about Cat. *I can't believe Cat did this to someone. It wasn't the woman I knew. Without a chain saw, it must have been tough cutting up Christopher's body. She had to be completely out of her mind when she did that.*

It was time to leave when the CSI guys arrived. He stood with his hand on the door. He shook his head.

I can't believe the amazing woman I worked with did this.

He stepped out of the doorway and closed the door on an unforgettable part of his life.

Chapter 27

Lee decided he should be the one to tell the swingers about Cat. What he wanted to discuss with them was toopersonal for them to find out from someone else.

Katrina, Hazel, and Anita gathered in Victor and Angela's apartment to meet with Lee. They sensed he was going to give them some bad news because of his demeanor.

"I thought you would like to know that I caught the person who killed Christopher Lockhart."

Hazel clasped her hands and said, "Thank God."

"I feel safer now," Anita declared.

Katrina took in a deep breath and announced, "Now I can go out again. I've been scared to death to venture outside."

Victor raised both thumbs in a triumphant gesture. "All right! Was it someone from the apartment complex?"

"No, in fact, I hate to tell you this. Cat killed him."

Anita's mouth fell open. "Cat? You mean your partner Cat?"

"That's exactly what I mean."

Everyone looked stunned. For a short time the room fell silent. The person who befriended them turned out to be a killer. It was a lot for each one of them to comprehend.

"Oh my God," Katrina groaned. "We considered her a friend. She deceived us."

"Why the hell did she kill him?" Hazel asked.

Lee replied, "I know you guys feel misled, but I want you to know she did it because he threatened you. In a way, she was looking out for you. That doesn't mean I condone what she did, but there's something else I think you should know. Cat used to be a swinger too."

Angela said, in her usual calm, sweet voice, "My gosh, I can't believe someone like that could get to be a detective.

"Well, no one knew. She never told anyone. She did tell *me* before they took her to the hospital after I shot her. Tore me up inside."

"Jesus, you shot her?" Victor yelled.

Lee stepped back and raised his hands, thinking for a few seconds what to say to them.

"We got into a gunfight before I saw who the killer was. Otherwise I would have just tried to make her give herself up. Believe me, she cared a lot about every one of you."

Victor shook his head. "But why didn't she just arrest him? Why kill and dismember him?"

"I guess only she knows the answer to that question, Vic. I don't know if we'll ever find out," Lee answered.

Katrina remarked, "Maybe she was involved in too many murder cases and simply lost it."

"Who knows," Lee said with a shrug.

Hazel placed a hand on Lee's shoulder and gave him a forgiving look. Everyone gathered close around him.

"We still think of her as a friend. Don't think too bad of her. She did what *she* thought was right."

"Yeah, I know. I *am* going to miss her. She was a great partner."

Victor rubbed his hand over his face. "I still can't believe she killed Christopher. We'll never forget her. She really was a friend."

Everyone agreed, even Lee.

Then Victor said, "Now, there's something we need to tell *you*. I heard that there might be another resident missing. This time it is a woman. Her name's Tamara Garrett. She's nineteen. She lives with her mother. Her mom says she didn't come home last night after she went to a friend's house for the day."

"Maybe she stayed all night at the friend's house and just hasn't come home yet," Lee responded.

"Her mother called and they told her she been there at all."

Lee took out a pad and wrote down everything they told him thus far.

Then he sat down and asked them more questions.

"Can you guys tell me a little about her?"

Hazel was the first to reply. "She seems like a real nice girl. Very friendly, but she isn't a swinger."

"She has long blonde hair, not her natural color. She has a great figure," Victor related.

Anita stated, "She has real long fingernails that are always well manicured. Each one of he nails has some kind of decoration."

"She has a boyfriend," Katrina commented, "but I don't know much about him."

"Could she have met up with him and stayed all night at his house?"

Anita informed Lee, "No, he lives here, at the other end of the hall. I saw him about three days ago and he told me he was going away to a conference for a week. He left yesterday morning."

"Besides, she would have called her mom. She was good about letting her know when she wasn't going to be home," Angela said.

Lee stood up to ask the last question before leaving. "Does she work?"

"No." Hazel said.

"Tell me what apartment she lives in. 'll start an investigation."

One by one the swingers gave him a hug and thanked him for telling them about Cat.

When Lee left, they continued discussing Cat.

Katrina said, "Can you believe Cat actually killed

someone? She just didn't seem like the type to do something like that."

Victor gave out a huge sigh and said, "You never know what people are capable of. If the circumstances were right, one of us might kill someone."

"I didn't even know Christopher threatened us," Hazel said with a shrug.

"I hope Lee gets a good partner," Victor said. "He's a very caring detective. You don't see that very often,"

Angela grabbed Victor's arm. "I can't believe someone else is missing. I hope she doesn't turn up dead like the others."

Chapter 28

Late afternoon on an eighty degree day, Maggie ventured out of the woods. Lee waited for her in the air conditioned restaurant across from the strip mall. He watched as she emerged from the trees and headed for the dumpster behind Safeway. He hurried to his car and drove around to the back of the building. He wanted to share important news with her.

When he drove up to the dumpster, she recognized the car. She turned her attention from the dumpster to meet the detective. Lee stopped the car. Maggie sauntered over to the driver's window. He rolled it down. She placed her arms on the edge and leaned in to talk.

"Hi Maggie, I have some good news for you. I caught the person who killed Christopher Lockhart. There won't be any more body parts in the dumpsters."

Maggie stood back from the car, surprised to finally hear some good news for a change. "Thank God! Who was it?"

"Well, this is the bad part of my news. It was my partner, Cat."

"Oh,for heavens sakes! Whatever possessed her ta do that? She seemed like such a nice lady." After thinking for a few seconds she asked, "Even if she *had* ta kill 'im 'cause he resisted arrest, why did she cut 'im up?"

"I don't know Maggie. We may never find out why." Better not to tell her the truth.

"Now I kin go ta the dumpsters without havin ta worry 'bout it anymore."

"Yes, so I hope you find lots of good stuff."

"Thank ya. Sorry ta hear 'bout Cat. I hope ya get a real good partner next time."

Lee and Maggie said their goodbyes and he left.

Maggie, thrilled about what Lee told her, couldn't wait to tell Peachie the news. She left her cart by the dumpster and scurried into the woods. Peachie, wearing the same dirty clothes she'd had on for a number of days, was taking a nap. She was tired and had decided not to go with Maggie to dumpster dive.

"Peachie, wake up! Wakeup!" Maggie said as she shook her friend. "I have something ta tell ya."

Rubbing her eyes, Peachie sat up. "Huh? What?"

"Lee just told me he caught Christopher Lockhart's killer. You'll never guess who it was."

"Who?" Peachie asked, still rubbing her eyes.

"His partner Cat."

"Ya gotta be kiddin. Cat, the detective?"

"Yeah, can ya believe it?"

"Christ, goes ta show ya how screwed up this world is. We's not as bad as everyone else."

When they finished discussing the bewildering news, Peachie decided to finish her nap since she knew Maggie no longer had to worry about finding a body part.

Maggie left for the dumpster. She still needed something for dinner. There was still lots of light left before the sun set behind the tall firs of the woods.

Maggie opened the lid on the dumpster and knew there was nothing to fear anymore. She enthusiastically dug into the huge metal container for treasures she was certain she would find.

The top layer gave up a box of cheese enchiladas, three Twinkies and four over ripe bananas.

"I can share the enchiladas with other people in the camp. Me and Peachie can eat the Twinkies and bananas," Maggie muttered as she placed them in her cart.

Ready to go back into the dumpster, she pulled her cart closer. She reached for a can of peaches but something else caught her attention. A package wrapped in some type of colored plastic lay close to the inside edge of the dumpster.

Visions of past dumpster finds entered her mind.

"This absolutely can't be what I'm thinkin it might be," Maggie mumbled.

She cautiously picked up the package. Examining the outside, she observed that it was covered with a dark blue plastic. Whoever wrapped it used an abundance of it and rolled it around the contents several times. It appeared to be two or three layers deep.

Maggie stopped looking at the package and closed her eyes. "Please God, don't let this be what it looks like."

Opening her eyes, she stared at what she held in her hand. "Don't be stupid. That would never happen ta you *three* times."

That's when Maggie noticed something dripping from the corner of the plastic. She let a drop of it land on an outstretched finger. Scrutinizing the drop, she surmised that it was blood. *Is this a piece of meat or a body part?*

She came to the conclusion that it *had* to be a piece of meat. Lee told her they recovered every part of Christopher's body. Feeling more confident, she began to peel back the plastic wrap. When it was half unrolled, Maggie stared at it for a few seconds. Then she dropped it into the dumpster, letting out a loud anguished scream.

Peachie, still in the woods, heard the scream. She recognized Maggie's voice and dashed out of the woods to see if she was okay. When she reached the dumpster, she saw Maggie standing next to it, her head buried in her hands. She was beside herself.

"Maggs, what's the matter?"

Maggie looked up with tears in her eyes.

"It's happened agin," she said as she pointed into the dumpster. "There's another body part in there. It's a woman's boob."

"How do ya know it's a woman's?"

"If it bulges and it's got a nipple on it, it's gotta be. I've seen enough women's bosoms ta know it's a woman."

"Okay, okay! I wonder why it's a woman this time? Jesus, how come they're still makin' sure *you* find 'em?"

"Don't know, but right now, wish I din't live here."

Peachie placed her hand on Maggie's shoulder and said, "We gotta call the cops, Maggs. Do ya know how ta get hold of that Lee fella?"

"Yeah," Maggie replied as she reached into her bra and brought out a piece of paper. "He gave me his cell phone number in case I ever needed ta call him. Can you do it? I'm so upset I don't know if I can."

"Hell, yah." Peachie took the paper Maggie held out to her. She found someone with a cell phone and called Lee Cummings.

Lee answered his phone to find another grisly case waiting for him on the other end.

Chapter 29

Lee couldn't believe what he heard when Peachie called him. He barely arrived home after telling Maggie the good news. Now he was being told Maggie found another body part. This time it wasn't from a male body.

A couple of days before the call from Peachie, the Chief called Lee into his office. "I want you to meet your new partner. This is Roxanne Watson."

Standing before him, he observed a woman who had a figure as good as Cat's, but she weighed a little more than Cat.

"Nice to meet you Roxanne. I suppose you already know about my former partner.

"Yes, I'm sorry it ended like that. By the way, everyone calls me Roxy. I'm new to the Jamesburg homicide squad. You'll be my first partner."

This would be their first big case together. He missed Cat, but put it in the back of his mind. Dwelling on it would not serve any useful purpose.

During their first meeting Lee filled her in about the swinger case.

Roxy had been shocked to hear about Cat being the second killer. "I assure you I won't be killing anyone unless necessary."

When Peachie called him, Lee called Roxy and told her to meet him at the police station. They drove to where Maggie and Peachie waited at the dumpster. The police had already cordoned off the area around the dumpster with crime scene tape.

Maggie ran up to Lee and grabbed his arm. "You said this wasn't' gonna happen agin."

Patting her arm, he said, "I'm so sorry Maggie, this is

definitely not part of the other cases. This is a copycat killer. By the way, this is my new partner Roxy."

Roxy shook Maggie's hand. "Nice to meet you."

"Whoever the killer is," Lee said, "he must know your routine. It's time to change your pattern."

Peachie blurted out, "If I could get my hands on the son of a bitch, I'd kill 'im for gettin Maggs so upset."

"Don't worry, we'll catch him", Lee replied. "Now let's see what you found."

Maggie was still too disturbed, therefore Peachie led them to the side of the dumpster where Maggie threw back the package. She leaned over and pointed. "There it is. Be careful, its leakin."

Lee reached in and lifted the plastic wrapped package. When he brought it over the edge of the dumpster he could see blood traveling around the edges of the package.

He said to one of the cops, "Hey, Henry. I don't know if you can get any prints from this plastic, but try before I un-wrap it."

While Henry tried getting any prints, Lee and Roxanne talked to Maggie and Peachie.

Roxanne said, "Maggie we'll work around the clock if necessary to catch this killer.

Lee, perplexed by another murder similar to the other two, said, "One of the differences is that the victim is female." Thinking about the missing woman from the swinger's apartment building, he said, "I may already know who the victim is."

Henry finished fingerprinting the package. He told Lee and Roxanne, "It's unlikely that I got anything useful from the plastic wrap. It looks like the killer wiped it pretty clean."

Lee picked up the package and opened it. It definitely turned out to be a female breast. He re-wrapped it and the detectives waited for Edward to arrive to examine the package contents and take it with him.

He arrived in a good mood as usual. When he saw Lee he shouted, "Oh my God. You guys just can't stay away from this kind of crap, can you?"

"Naw, we're just like you. That's why we see you so often, Ed," Lee quipped.

Motioning for the Medical Examiner to come closer, Lee turned him to face his new partner.

"Ed, this is Roxanne Watson. We all call her Roxy."

The sun glistened off her dark brown hair and cast splinters of sparkle.

Edward held out his hand and shook Roxy's while thinking *What a hottie.* He looked at Lee and said, "Let's hope she doesn't get as *involved* in the case as Cat did," winking before he let go of Roxy's hand.

Lee replied, "I think she's too smart for that. Hopefully, there are not two female detectives like that."

"Besides," Roxy came back with, "I wouldn't want a detective as clever as Lee, figuring out I was the killer and arresting me."

When Edward left, Lee and Roxy talked some more with Maggie and Peachie.

Roxy asked Maggie, "When you arrived, did you see or hear anything suspicious such as a car parked nearby or anyone on foot?"

"No, I din't see nothin or nobody."

She asked Peachie, "Did you see anything suspicious when you arrived?"

"No, nuttin. Just Maggs, standin there cryin."

Maggie turned to Lee, "Why does this keep happenin to me?"

"I don't know why someone is killing and dismembering a victim again, but I'm guessing someone knows exactly what dumpster you are going to hit next.

Stop putting your cart out the night before. They must drive around until they see your cart every night."

Maggie nodded an okay. "I'll do it your way from now on."

Peachie said, "Let's go home, Maggs. I'll share my food wit you tonight."

"You got it! Let's go."

While they drove back to the police station, Lee said, "I think you should do most of the talking if we encounter Maggie again. I don't think she has much trust in me anymore."

Roxy replied, "Yeah, I kinda get that feeling too. Okay, if we meet again, I'll try to steer the conversation my way."

They both hoped there wouldn't be any more of those meetings, but they assumed there would be.

Chapter 30

He hadn't planned on killing her. However, she told him unless he left his wife, she was going to tell her about their affair. They spent the whole day together. She told her mother she was spending time with a friend. It ended at one of the local motels frequented by prostitutes.

The manager, Calvin, was grubby looking. Part of his dirty, dark brown hair was plastered to his head while other parts stuck out. He always looked like he just tumbled out of bed.

He wasn't about to pay for a high class motel for a little sex with a woman he really didn't care about.

When they lay nestled in each others arms, she said, "I love you."

He replied, "I love you too."

That's when she asked, "How soon are you going to ask your wife for a divorce?"

Divorce?

He never told her he wanted to leave his wife. He saw her several times, but only for fun and sex.

Why had she pushed him about divorcing his wife?

It started when he told her, "I have no intention of ever leaving her."

She leapt out of bed and started pacing. First she cried. Then she screamed at him. Suddenly she seemed to calm down. "I'm going to tell you wife about our sexual encounters if you don't leave her."

He panicked. "I love my wife." *I can't let this happen.* He told her again, "I am *not* leaving her."

She slapped him. "You'll be sorry when I tell her about our affair.

That's when he lost it! He grabbed hold of her neck

with both hands and started squeezing. She fought back violently. She tried to scream. No sound came out of her throat. She hit him with her fists. She scratched him as hard as she could. She tried to kick him in the groin.

Somehow he managed to keep his stranglehold on her neck. He hadn't realized how hard and long and he squeezed until her body dropped to the floor. Suddenly he let go of her neck.

She didn't move. Feeling for a pulse and finding none, he knew she was dead.

He was overwhelmed with fear. Trembling, he broke out into a cold sweat. That's when he thought about his predicament. *I can't become hysterical. I need to calm down and try to think of what to do.*

He couldn't call the police since he was the person who'd killed her. That was *not* the thing to do. *Okay, think! Think!*

Then he remembered about the swinger and the guy at the apartment building where he lived that had been murdered. Their killers cut up the bodies and threw the parts into dumpsters. The only problem was, he didn't have any place to cut up the body. He'd have to find someplace.

He waited until there was no one in the motel parking lot. Then he opened his trunk and cautiously carried the body to the car. He stuffed it in the trunk. Taking everything of his and hers, he left the motel room.

He sat in his car for a few minutes trying to think of where he could cut up her body. *First, have I got anything to do it with?* He pictured his trunk. *Yes, I have a chainsaw. Plus I have some raingear in my trunk I wear to hunt in when it's raining.*

Then it suddenly came to him where he could do the job. Starting his car, he drove out of the parking lot and onto the highway. Approximately ten minutes later, he arrived at his destination in a dense forest area not far from Jamesburg.

It's not dark yet, so the noise from my chainsaw shouldn't alarm anyone. They'll just think it's someone cutting down trees.

He opened the trunk and looked at her. *You made a mistake when you threatened to tell my wife about us. I'm a happily married man. Did you really think I would leave my wife for a slut like you?*

After lifting the body out of the trunk, he carried it deep into the woods. Then he returned to the car and put on the raingear. Taking the chainsaw out of the trunk, he went back to where he left the body. He undressed her and laid the clothes in a heap by the chainsaw.

Okay, where should I start? Head, legs, arms, hands or feet? I think I'll do the legs first.

He lifted the chainsaw and started cutting the right leg. A sickening feeling came over him and he had to stop for a minute. Since the blood hadn't clotted yet, blood spurted out of the cut. Some of it landed on his raingear and some on the ground and bushes nearby. When he finished cutting, he laid the leg on the ground and cut off the left leg, laying it next to first one. He did the arms next, then the hands and feet.

Stopping to rest, he realized the raingear was covered in blood. Luckily he wore a pair of gloves he found in his trunk. The raingear and gloves kept him from getting blood on his clothes and hands. He did have some on his face and in his hair.

I'll stop somewhere and wash my face and hair before I go home. Right now, back to work.

The last part to be cut was the head. He picked up the chainsaw and started cutting. Since it had been long enough after her death, the blood had started clotting.

There was none squirting out. He was thankful for that. Cutting her head off nearly made him puke.

When he finished cutting up the body, he looked at his watch. *It's not dark yet. I still have time to buy stuff to wrap the parts in.*

He took off the gloves and raingear and tossed it on the pile of clothes. *I need to buy something to put this stuff in.*

While getting into the car, he looked in the mirror at his face and hair. He noticed spots of blood on his cheek and forehead. He also felt some blood in his hair. The trip to the store was interrupted by a stop at a gas station restroom. When he washed the blood from his face, he stopped and looked at himself in the mirror. He wasn't sure he was looking at the same man with a loving wife and children. The man in the mirror was a beast who had just killed and chopped up a woman. The killer took a huge breath, closed his eyes for a few seconds, then turned out the light and left the bathroom.

It didn't take long to buy what he needed at the store. When he returned to the horrifying scene he'd created, he packaged the body parts in plastic wrap and put them in the trunk. Then he threw the gloves, raingear and her clothes in a large plastic bag and also tossed it into the trunk.

He sat in the front seat of his car for a while until he composed himself enough to start the car. Then he drove home, anxious to see his wife and children.

The long sleeves on his shirt hid the scratches on his arms. They hurt like hell. Hopefully his wife would never notice them.

The next morning, he took a package out of the freezer and since he had heard about the dumpster diver's routine, he simply checked where she left her cart. He drove up to the dumpster. Waiting a while to make sure no one was in the area, he eventually stepped out of his car and opened the trunk. Retrieving the package, he walked over to the dumpster. He looked around for a few seconds, then lifted the package and threw it inside. Getting back into his car, he leaned back and gave out a huge sigh of relief.

When he checked where the dumpster diver's cart was after she found the first package, he found out her routine changed. It was okay. It didn't matter. He needed to get rid of every package right away before his wife started asking questions about the lock on the freezer. What he decided to do wouldn't make any difference whatever the dumpster diver changed to. She would find a package anyway.

That night, he was already in bed when Evelyn, his wife, slipped into bed. Despite her salt and pepper grey hair, she was as beautiful as ever. She had a face like an angel and a figure as good as when he first met her.

"What's the lock on the freezer for?"

Oh my God, think fast.

"I noticed the latch on it wasn't working very well, so I put a lock on it. I'll buy a new one tomorrow and replace the old one."

That seemed to satisfy her curiosity.

The next morning, he called in sick again. He said to Evelyn, "There's some things we need at the grocery store. Can you go get them while I get a new latch for the freezer?"

While she was gone, he removed the rest of the packages from the freezer and put them in the trunk of his car. Then he drove to every dumpster where Maggie left her cart and dropped at least one of the packages into every one of them. That left the other half of the body to dispose of the following day. It was cold enough in his trunk for one more day.

The last place gave him a real scare. When he was behind the store, an employee from the store came out and saw him toss a package into the dumpster.

He yelled, "Hey, this dumpster is for store use. You're not supposed to be throwing stuff in it."

"Oh, sorry. I won't do it again."

He drove off and watched in his rear view mirror. The employee threw something into the dumpster and went back into the store.

Thank God, he didn't check to see what I flung in there.

He was close to coming unglued as he drove home. If that employee had stopped him and checked what it was he tossed in the dumpster, he could have been a dead duck. When he was close to home, he calmed down as much as he could.

Evelyn met him at the door when he arrived home. "I see you took the lock off the freezer."

"Yes, I changed the latch. It works good now."

"Where did you go after you got done with that?"

"One of my old buddies called and wanted to go have a drink. You weren't home yet, so I decided to go."

Evelyn took his hand and led him to the sofa. She sat down with him and put her arms around him. She gave him a hug and a kiss. "You've had a long day. I'll fix you a nice dinner."

When she stood, he looked at her and smiled. *Why do I keep trying to find something better than this?*

Chapter 31

Maggie and Peachie relaxed in the shade of the fir trees at the homeless camp. The excessive heat of the past few days made it impossible to dumpster dive until late afternoon.

Maggie announced, "Lee said I needed ta change my routine. I'm not gonna leave my cart at the dumpster I want ta dive in from now on."

"That's good," Peachie said, nodding. "No more body parts. What time ya gonna go ta the dumpster?"

"I think 'bout seven this evenin. It's too hot ta go sooner. I can't handle the heat."

"At least since yur not gonna leave yur cart at the dumpsters anymore, the killer won't know which dumpster yur gonna dive in. But just in case, why don't I go wit ya. I'll be there ta support ya in case ya do find anudder body part."

Placing her hand on her forehead, Maggie said, "Thank God. I don't think I could stand finding another part of a body. I would be happy ta have ya along."

Maggie and Peachie talked most of the afternoon. Then they decided to take a nap. They wanted to be rested for their foraging evening.

Around seven o'clock, they set out to the dumpster Maggie chose. It was the first time in many days she felt good about going out diving. Assured by Lee that she would not be encountering any body parts, she had a cheerful outlook for the evening exploration.

When they arrived at the dumpster, Maggie pushed her cart close to it. She left it in front of the huge metal container while she looked for something to stand on. A large wooden box came into view. She shoved it to the front of the dumpster. Suddenly, she stopped and looked at Peachie.

"What's the matter Maggs?"

"I'm scared. What if I do find another body part? I don't think I could stand it."

"Do ya want *me* ta rummage through the dumpster and *you* put the stuff inta the cart?"

"Would ya? I'm too freaked out ta do it."

"Sure," Peachie replied. "I kin take anythin."

Peachie climbed onto the box and began to search the contents of the dumpster for goodies. The large variety of food she saw made her excited. There was bread and lunch meat, potato chips, several jars of jelly plus crackers and Twinkies. She thought she'd died and gone to Heaven.

"Shit, Maggs, we hit the mother-load!"

Maggie quickly loaded the cart with everything Peachie handed her. She felt absolutely ecstatic.

That was only the first layer of food.

Peachie started pushing aside everything she didn't want in the dumpster. The second layer proved to be as profitable as the first one. Peachie gazed upon hot dogs and hot dog buns waiting for her to pick them up as if they had been placed there only for her to find. Cans of expired baked beans greeted her eyes next. They only recently expired. She knew they would still be good.

"You and me are gonna have a party, Maggs," she nearly shouted. "I'm happy as a clam taday." It's the best dumpster I've dived inta for a long time."

While Maggie placed the items in the cart, she said, "Yeah, everything seems okay. No body parts!"

Peachie kept digging and came across the best find yet. Deep inside, she found two expired cakes.

"Holy cow, Maggs," she said as she lifted both cakes out and handed them to Maggie. "We kin share these wit our friends at the camp."

Maggie felt joyful as she looked at the cart which began to look quite full. The fear she'd had dissipated.

Peachie, feeling there had to be more good stuff, continued looking in the dumpster. Deep inside, she found a package wrapped in dark blue plastic wrap.

"Oh, Oh, Maggs! Look at this. Peachie lifted the package out of the dumpster and showed it to Maggie.

Instantly, the euphoria Maggie experienced vanished as she recognized the wrapping. She burst out crying. "It can't be! Lee told me there wouldn't be anymore body parts. But I'm positive ya found another one. Put it back and see if ya kin find someone with a cell phone so ya kin call Lee." She gave Peachie Lee's phone number.

Peachie left her now completely unglued friend to find someone who would let her use their cell phone. When she found a person generous enough, she dialed the number Maggie gave her. When Lee answered, Peachie said, "Yur not gonna believe this, but I am dumpster divin with Maggie. She was afraid to get into the dumpster, so I did it for her. We think I found another body part in it. Maggie's really upset."

Lee said, "I'm leaving right now. I'll be there in a few minutes. Try to keep Maggie calm til I get there."

Peachie returned to where Maggie sat on the box, tears streaming down her face.

Lee arrived in minutes like he said he would. Maggie was still crying. "How did he know which dumpster I was gonna go ta? I didn't put my cart there."

"I don't know Maggie," Lee answered. Try to calm down. He turned to Peachie. "Show me what you found."

While she led Lee to the dumpster, Peachie said, "How could the bastard do this ta her agin? I'd like ta kill *him* and cut *him* up inta little pieces."

Peering into the dumpster, Lee also surmised there was another body part there.

Several police cars showed up after Lee called. The cops placed crime scene tape around the dumpster area.

Lee and Peachie resumed trying to calm the extremely upset Maggie.

Roxy arrived shortly after Lee called her. She was able to calm Maggie a little more. When Maggie was composed enough to talk, Roxy and Lee sat down and entered into a life changing conversation with her.

Roxy started by saying, "Maggie, you need someplace to live so you won't have to be homeless anymore."

Lee added, "This is no way that a woman your age should be living. We would like to see you have someplace to live besides the streets."

Maggie nodded her head. "I think you're right," she agreed. I *do* need a place to live, but I don't have any money ta pay for it."

"Don't worry," Roxy replied. "We know of someplace you can go. They will help you get someplace to live."

"We want to take you to a homeless shelter we know of," Lee said. They will take good care of you and get you a permanent home. I've worked with them before."

Maggie readily agreed. It was time to have someplace to live. No more body parts!

They ended the conversation just as the Medical Examiner arrived. He would have sent his assistant, but he wanted to see Roxy and Lee again. He was his usual jovial self.

Edward looked at Lee and said, "You again? I can't seem to get rid of you."

"You love us and you know it," Lee remarked.

"You could at least give me a whole body. You keep giving me bits and pieces."

Roxy butted in with, "We love you or we wouldn't give you anything. We keep you in business."

Edward laughed. "So what you got this time? My guess is another body part."

Lee raised his hands and shrugged. "Well, you're right. We think it *is* another body part. Take a look."

Lee motioned towards the dumpster. He picked the package up and gave it to Edward. It had already been checked for prints. The Medical Examiner opened it.

First he saw a finger. He continued to undo the package. When the rest of the wrapping fell away, a complete hand came into view.

Edward looked at Lee and said, "If you need a hand with anything, I happen to have an extra one."

"Leave it to you Ed. I knew you'd come up with something funny to say."

"Sorry, can't help myself. It just comes naturally."

Edward re-wrapped the package and left, taking it with him.

Roxy and Peachie stayed with Maggie to keep her spirits up while Lee finished what he needed at the scene.

Lee ordered every dumpster in the city to be checked for body parts. He had done this as part of each investigation when Maggie found body parts. However, none were ever found in any of the other dumpsters.

When Lee finished his part of the investigation, they drove Maggie and Peachie to the homeless camp. They picked up Maggie's belongings. Then Maggie gave Peachie a hug and said goodbye.

Lee and Roxy escorted Maggie to the homeless shelter they told her about. They introduced Maggie to the head of the homeless shelter when they arrived. They left her in the hands of their friend and said goodbye. The three of them hoped it would be the last time they would see her as part of a murder investigation.

Chapter 32

Skip Howell, to put it mildly, was a loosely put together kid. Still trying to get out of the child stage at fourteen, he and his friend Alva Worthington had a lot of adventures that could be considered on the childish side. Alva was thirteen but she was for the most part, more grown up than Skip.

It was a beautiful sunny day when they decided to ride their bikes into the woods to see what exciting things they might find there. The sun was high in the sky and shot rays of warmth to each of them. Alva stopped her bike at the edge of the fir lined area they frequented before she entered the woods. Skip followed suit. Alva stepped off the pedals of her bike and, closing her eyes, turned her face toward the warmth that enveloped her.

"The sun feels good. I hope the animals are out today," Alva remarked.

"Yeah, it's a nice day. They should be."

They both enjoyed watching the wildlife in the forest. They loved seeing the squirrels flittering up and down the trees. They brought food to feed them. Some of them came right up to Skip and Alva for the handouts they held out. Even several deer had become used to seeing them and took food out of their outstretched hands.

Leaving their bikes a little inside the woods so they wouldn't be stolen, they excitedly walked deep into the forest. Along the way, they noticed a couple of squirrels chasing each other around some of the trees. They had a feeling it was going to be a good day.

Suddenly, as Skip entered a small clearing, Alva grabbed his arm and pulled him back. "It looks like there's something on the ground. I hope I'm wrong, but it looks like blood."

"What?" Skip responded, unsure if he heard her correctly. "Can't be."

Bending down to take a closer look, Alva replied, "There is blood here."

"Some hunter must have killed a deer here," Skip said, stepping closer to the area to get a better look.

"Then he must have butchered it here too because there's blood everywhere. It's on the ground and on the trees and bushes. What if it wasn't a hunter? Maybe somebody killed someone here."

"*You* think somebody died here?" Skip said as he took a tissue from his pocket and cleaned some blood off his shoe. "*I* think it was a hunter killing a deer."

"But what if it wasn't? We should find out for sure. *I* think we should call the police."

Skip answered in a huff, "Okay, let's call the cops." He pulled a cell phone out of his pocket and was going to dial 911 but he said to Alva, "I can't get a signal. See if you can on your phone."

Alva pulled her cell phone out of her pocket and tried to get a signal. She wasn't successful in getting one either. They picked up their bikes and rode to the nearest place they could finally get a signal.

Skip dialed 911. When the operator asked what his emergency was, he said, "Me and a friend were out in the woods and found a place where there's lots of blood. We don't know if it's from a human or an animal. Can you send someone out here to check it out?" He gave her the approximate area where they called from.

A few minutes later, a police car came into sight with its lights flashing and siren blaring. Skip and Alva flagged them down. The cops followed them into the woods.

Two cops accompanied them to where they found the blood. When they observed how large the area was, one of them went back to the cop car and brought two pairs of plastic boots to put over their shoes.

They had been looking over the area for any evidence of a crime for a while. Suddenly one of them held up something. It was a necklace. He said, "Looks like someone *might* have been killed here."

One of the cops spoke to Skip and Alva. "You need to go home now. It does look like a crime scene. You can't be here anymore. There will be other people coming to investigate. Will you write your names, addresses and phone numbers on this pad, please?"

When they left, Alva said to Skip, "See, I told you somebody could have been killed here. It's a good thing you listened to me this time."

Skip was heard saying to Alva, "Yeah, Yeah. This time you were right. But you're not right every time." They hurried home to tell their moms about their find.

The cops cordoned off the area with crime scene tape and notified the police chief to send out someone to investigate a possible murder.

Chapter 33

The hot afternoon sun felt like a thousand bombs exploding on the surface of Lee's skin. He couldn't wait to get inside the air conditioned restaurant. He and Roxy had confirmed the murder victim's identity. Lee surmised who it would turn out to be since talking to the swingers. Tamara Garrett was indeed the victim. Once inside the restaurant, they discussed the case.

Roxy asked Lee, "Do you think there is any connection to the swingers?"

"I don't know, I can't think of any possible connection to them. However, I think we should talk to the swingers to see if there might be one."

"I concur, she said. We should have a talk with them to find out if there could be."

"Maybe they've heard information that could help us even if there isn't any connection to them."

When they finished their lunch, Lee and Roxy set out for the swinger's apartment building. The first one they talked to was Katrina.

"Did you know Tamara?" Roxy asked.

"I met her a couple of times. She was always at the parties that the owner of the apartments gave. I never really had a conversation with her. I probably shouldn't say this about her since she's dead, but she did a lot of flirting with the guys at the parties. Maybe someone's wife got jealous and killed her."

"It's a possibility," Roxy said. "No woman wants another woman coming on to their husband."

Lee asked, "Did she ever flirt with your husband?"

"Come to think of it, no. Maybe she knew Anita was already having an affair with *my* husband."

There was no other information Katrina could give them. They moved on to Anita's apartment.

Anita didn't answer her door right away. Lee and Roxy could hear a flurry of activity through the paper thin door.

Roxy whispered to Lee, "Either she is cleaning up a messy room or she has a visitor who needs to skeedaddle to the bedroom."

Lee laughed and replied, "My guess is it's someone who doesn't want to be seen."

When Anita opened the door, she was dressed only in a nightgown. Roxy threw a quick glance at Lee. The look on his face told a story. He tipped his head a teeny bit as if to say, "I think we can tell what's going on here."

Roxy gave him a smile that said she agreed.

A surprised expression crossed Anita's face when she saw them. "Oh, hi. How come you guys are here again? I thought your murder cases were solved?"

"Those *were* solved," Lee replied. We have a *new* one. The woman who was missing is dead. Someone murdered Tamara Garrett. Did you know her?"

"As a matter of fact, I did. She was sort of like me. She preferred dating married men. If you don't want to get into a commitment of any kind, it's the thing to do."

"So you're telling us that she dated married men?"

"Yeah, I know one that she dated. He is definitely married. I dated him too."

"What is his name and address?" Roxy asked.

"His name is Kevin Forester. He lives in the Highlands. He has a big home and a wife who thinks he is a saint." Anita snickered. "If only she knew he'll go to bed with any woman who smiles at him! She doesn't drive, so she can't follow him if she suspects anything."

She gave them Kevin's address. Then she asked, "Is that all you need from me? I'm kind of busy. I have something I need to do."

Lee replied, "Yup, we're done. Thanks for the information."

When the door to the apartment closed, Lee said, "I bet I know what Anita needed to do."

Roxy gave him a little smirk. "I think it was pretty obvious what was going on. Judging from what she said, I'd wager he's a married man."

"Our killer could possibly be Kevin Forester. I doubt that it's his wife since Anita said she doesn't drive."

When they left Anita's apartment, Roxy remarked, "Let's put Forester on a list of possible suspects."

Next Lee and Roxy visited Hazel since Victor wouldn't be home from work yet.

Hazel was cooperative, but had little to tell them. "I knew who Tamara was, but I never talked to her. Since Joseph killed Manny, I don't have much to do with anyone from here, so I haven't heard any scuttlebutt. Do you think someone from here killed Tamara?"

"We don't know. It could have been anyone from anywhere," Lee replied.

Looking at his watch, Lee noticed that Victor should be home.

"Well," Roxy said, "We have to talk to Victor and Angela yet. We'll let you know if we need to talk again."

"Sorry I couldn't be more help."

Lee said, "Maybe Victor and Angela can give us something to help us find the killer."

When they arrived at Victor and Angela's apartment, Victor stood in the doorway waiting for them.

"Hey guys, Hazel called and said you were coming."

Lee asked, "Did she tell you why we're here?"

"No, what's up?"

Roxy answered Victor's question, "The woman you told us about is dead. We're investigating her death."

"I take it she was murdered."

"Yes," Lee replied, "just like the other victims. She has been cut up into pieces. The dumpster diver has found two of the body parts."

"My God!" Victor said, disbelief showing on his face. It couldn't be connected to us. She wasn't part of us."

"Did you know her?" Roxy asked.

"No, I only saw her at our parties. She was single so she made the rounds of all the single men *plus* some of the married ones."

"Who told you she disappeared?" Lee asked as Victor shook his head.

"Norman Templeman. We were talking about the other murders and he told me Tamara had disappeared."

"When was that?" Lee asked, hoping that if it was early enough, he might be a good suspect.

Victor replied, "He discussed Tamara's disappearance the day after she went missing."

Lee and Roxy talked with Victor for awhile. He could not give them any more information.

When they left Victor and Angela's apartment, they discussed Norman Templeman.

"I think he is a possible suspect, said Lee. He knew Tamara disappeared before anyone else."

"I agree, I think he's someone we should consider."

Lee commented that they should also investigate Kevin Forester. Roxy agreed.

Now at least they had a couple of possible suspects. It was time to investigate them.

Chapter 34

Lee and Roxy decided to investigate Norman Templeman first. He lived in the same apartment complex as the victim. First they found out as much information about him as possible. They started by interviewing other residents who knew him. Only one of them seemed to know the most about him.

According to Jacob Rhodes, he considered Norman to be his best friend.

"He's a good guy. I've known him for eight years. He's been married for five years."

"Is it a happy marriage?" asked Roxy.

"Oh yeah! He never says anything bad about his wife. He calls her his fairy princess."

"Do you know if Tamara flirted with him?" Lee asked. "That she came on to him?"

Jacob laughed, "Tamara flirted with everybody. I doubt if there are any men here that she didn't flirt with."

"Did you ever *see* her flirt with him?"

"Yes, as a matter of fact, I saw her sit in his lap, right in front of his wife."

Roxy, thinking *that* sounded interesting, inquired, "Do you think they could have had an affair?"

"Heck, no! This man really loves his wife. They are a very happy couple."

"Do you know," Lee asked, "*how* he knew *when* she disappeared?"

"No he didn't tell me how he knew it."

None of the other residents knew either. Unable to gain any useful information Lee and Roxy discussed what their next move should be over lunch.

Lee started the conversation. "Even though this guy

seems to have a good marriage, he could have had an affair with Tamara. We should probably bring him in for questioning."

"I have a better idea. I think we should follow both of our possible suspects for awhile. If one of them is our killer, he may lead us to the rest of the body."

"That sounds like a great idea," Lee said. "Kevin Forester owns a home. He could have a place to chop someone up, but Norman Templeton doesn't. If he did that in his apartment, his wife would know it. If he's the killer, he must have another place to do it in."

"It's possible she does know it and is too scared to tell the police."

Lee said, "The same thing could be true of Kevin Forester's wife if he is the killer. Maybe we should bring both wife's in and question them."

"I think we should follow the guys first. If we don't get anywhere with that, then we can bring the wives in."

When they finished lunch, Lee and Roxy drove to the apartment complex to talk to Jacob.

Lee asked him, "Do you know what kind of car Norman drives?"

"Yeah," he replied, "it's a 2003 Kia. It's a medium grey color."

"Do you know if he's home right now?"

Jacob looked out the window. "Yes, he's home. That's his car right down there." He quickly turned to Lee and asked, "You don't think he's the one who killed Tamara do you?"

"We're just doing a thorough investigation. We don't know who killed her."

The detectives thanked Jacob and left. They parked their car in a place where they could see if Norman came out to his car and drove away.

The stakeout had begun.

Shortly after they started watching Norman's car for activity, Lee's phone rang. The call ended with a puzzled look on his face.

"I was just told that when the rest of Maggie's dumpsters were checked, they all had one body part in them. Ed said when he put them together, there is still a lot of the body to be recovered. For some reason, the killer got rid of more than one body part at a time."

Roxy exclaimed, "Oh my God, if he gets rid of the rest at one time, we might not be able to catch him in the act. I hope one of these guys is our killer. Otherwise, this is going to be a long investigation. At least next time, Maggie won't have to find any more body parts."

Lee placed a hand on Roxy's shoulder. "It just occurred to me. I think I know why he put one body part in each of Maggie's dumpsters. Since she changed her routine, he didn't know which one to put a body part in, so he put one in each dumpster. He knew that way she'd find one of them."

"I think you're right, that means he will be doing the same thing probably tomorrow morning since he doesn't know Maggie won't be dumpster diving any more. We can catch him dumping a body part at one of Maggie's dumpsters in the morning."

"Yup," Lee acknowledged, "What are we sitting here for? All we have to do is be there at the time the trash guy empties the dumpster and wait for our killer to arrive. It won't matter which dumpster we stakeout, he will probably go to all of them."

Chapter 35

Lee and Roxy felt confident they could nab the killer at one of the dumpsters. When they left Norman Templeman's apartment complex, they needed to discuss the next step in the investigation. They decided to hash out the details over dinner.

They arrived at the restaurant a little after six o'clock. The discussion started as soon as they finished ordering.

Roxy began by asking, "Which dumpster should we stakeout?"

"I think the one behind the Safeway store by the homeless camp is a good one. There are several places where we can watch without being seen."

"I agree, it would be a good place. What time does the trash collection truck get there?"

"I'm not sure," Lee answered. Since we don't have time to check it out, I think we should be there by four o'clock tomorrow morning."

"Sounds good to me."

"I hope we're right about this guy. I want the killings at that place to be over. I'm ready for a new assignment."

"Me too," Roxy said, "maybe something less gory than cutting someone up. A normal murder would at least be less horrifying."

Dinner arrived as Lee told Roxy, "I'll pick you up about 3:30 in the morning."

Roxy drew a rough drawing of the area and pointed to a spot near the dumpster. "I think this would be a good place for us to hide so he won't see us."

"I agree," Lee replied.

When they finished dinner, Lee took Roxy home. They both needed a good night's rest for what might happen when they encountered the killer. Hopefully he would surrender peacefully. However, both of them needed to be sharp in case it turned out to be a stand off.

The next morning, Roxy anticipated their encounter with a killer. She held her empty gun in one hand and wrapped the fingers of the other hand around her wrist. Closing her eyes, she squeezed the trigger. Spending a few seconds praying they would be safe, she took in a deep breath and let it out slowly.

A knock on the door brought her thoughts back to reality. When she opened it, Lee stood there.

"You ready to do this?" he asked.

"As ready as I'll ever be," she answered.

"Okay, let's go."

Roxy thought the trip to Safeway seemed way too short. Neither of them said anything until Lee found a good spot to park where they could see the dumpster without being seen themselves.

Roxy turned to Lee and said, "I've never shot anyone. Have you?"

Lee looked at Roxy and suddenly realized her face showed fear. He never saw an expression like that on her face before.

"Yeah," he replied. "Cat and I once cornered a perp who shot at us. I shot him in the chest. He died the next day. They said it was justifiable."

"It must be hard to shoot someone."

"Not really. You don't have time to think about it. It happens in a split second. If you took time to think about it, you could be the dead one yourself."

Roxy gave him a quick, *What am I doing here?* glance and took a short breath.

"I guess you're right. I hope I won't have to find out this morning."

"If anything like that happens, don't think about it.

Just shoot!"

The trash guy finally arrived at forty seven minutes after four. Streaks of sunlight began what promised to be a long hot day.

It wasn't more than a few minutes after the garbage truck left that a dark blue car pulled up at one end of the dumpster.

"He's here!" Lee yelled, simultaneously starting the car. They watched as a man exited the car and tossed something into the dumpster.

Lee threw the car into first gear and gunned it. He came to a screeching halt in front of the dumpster. He and Roxy flung open their doors. Roxy started to run behind the car as Lee shouted at the fleeing suspect.

"Stop, you're under arrest!"

The answer came in the form of a bullet. It grazed her arm. Roxy screamed as she rounded the car. She aimed with her right hand while holding her injured arm.

Seeing Lee's concerned face, she said, "I'm okay. It's only my arm."

Cautiously looking over the car, Lee said, "One of us needs to get behind him, but he's right up against that wall. I can see only one way. Cover me," he said as he sprang into action.

Roxy shot at the suspect as Lee ran out from the side of the car. She kept shooting until Lee disappeared around the corner of the building. She reloaded as quickly as she could.

Lee vanished for a long time. The suspect and Roxy exchanged shots several times before Lee showed up. He suddenly appeared on the roof of the building. He raised his gun and pointed it at the suspect.

"Put your hands up."

"Piss on you!" the suspect yelled and raised his gun faster than Lee could pull the trigger.

There was no time to react before the shot rang out. Lee heard it and flinched. Feeling no pain, he looked at the suspect. A look of disbelief came over his face.

The suspect fell to the ground.

He saw Roxy standing out in the open, her gun still pointed at the suspect.

Lee bolted off the roof as fast as he could. When he rounded the building, Roxy still aimed her gun at the suspect, even though he wasn't moving.

"It's okay Roxy. I'm here," Lee reassured her.

He put his hand on hers and lowered the hand *and* the gun. Then he checked the wound on Roxy's arm. He was surprised that it simply looked like a scratch.

"It's not bad. Some antibiotic cream and a band aid will probably be all you'll need."

"Is he dead?"

He bent over and felt for a pulse.

"No, he's still alive," Lee answered as he dialed 911 for the police and an ambulance.

Lee guided Roxy to the car. She sat on the drivers side, still holding the gun in her hand. "Uh, you can put the gun away now, Roxy. Thank you for saving my life."

She snapped out of her stupor. "Oh, your welcome. Thank heavens it's over."

Curiosity overcame Lee. He walked over to the suspect and checked his pockets. He found the wallet. After looking at the suspect's driver's license, he went over to Roxy.

"It's Kevin Forester."

The ambulance and police arrived at basically the same time. The paramedics worked on Kevin getting him stable enough to transport to the hospital. One of them also tended to Roxy's arm.

When he finished bandaging her arm, he told Lee, "She won't have to go to the hospital. It's just a crease. It should heal okay without any problem."

Lee joined Roxy. "You're lucky. No hospital."

"I'm fine," she replied.

Lee talked to one of the cops who had been at the other dumpster finds. "I think if we look in this dumpster, we'll find another body part."

When they looked, Lee found the package he knew contained a part of Tamara's body. He ordered a search of the rest of Maggie's dumpsters.

The paramedics stabilized Kevin enough to transport him to the hospital. He was conscious as they carried him to the ambulance. He asked them to stop as they passed Lee.

"I killed her because she was going to tell my wife about our affair."

"Well, your wife is going to know about her now."

Lee and Roxy talked while they waited for the Medical Examiner to arrive.

Roxy said, "I can't believe I shot him. You were right. It was automatic. I didn't even have time to think about it. So fast."

Lee put his hand on her shoulder and in a Humphrey Bogart voice said, "I knew you could do it kid."

Chapter 36

The investigation lasted longer than Lee and Roxy anticipated. They knew the main question to be addressed would be to find out where Kevin cut up Tamara's body. The rest of the body parts had been found in the dumpsters Lee ordered to be searched.

Their first action resulted in a search warrant for Kevin's home. When they arrived at the house, his wife met them and the forensics team. She already knew her husband killed Tamara and cut her body into parts. They could tell she had been doing a lot of crying.

Roxy said, "We're sorry Mrs. Forester. We are probably going to tear your house apart. We are going to look for evidence."

Evelyn replied, "Go ahead and do whatever you need to do. Tear it all to hell if you want to. I'm putting it up for sale soon anyway. I can't live here anymore. I feel like killing my husband and disposing of him the same way he did his mistress."

They thoroughly searched the house and every outbuilding. They discovered no sign of someone killing or cutting up a body anywhere on the grounds.

Lee asked Evelyn, "Do you own any other structure where he could have dismembered the body?"

"No, we don't own anything else, at least, not that I know of."

Lee called a towing company and ordered a second car Kevin owned.

When they left the Forester home, Lee said, "Well, I guess it's time to talk to Kevin."

While he drove to the hospital, he said, "Either his wife never knew about it or he rented something."

Roxy replied, "I just hope he admits to having a place where he butchered her."

Kevin Forester sat up in bed, awake and coherent enough to question. Unfortunately, they wouldn't like his answers.

Lee started by asking, "Where did you cut up Tamara's body?"

"I never cut up anyone's body."

"What? You already told me you killed her, Kevin."

"I never killed anyone and I never told you I did."

"Why did you shoot at us if you didn't kill anyone?"

"I thought you were holding me up."

"I told you that you were under arrest before you started shooting."

"I didn't hear you say that, and I want a lawyer here if you want to ask me any more questions."

With clenched teeth, close to Kevin's face, Lee replied, "Okay Kevin, we can do this the hard way."

"That bastard told me he killed her," Lee said when they were leaving the hospital. "He was going to tell his wife about their affair."

Roxy placed a hand on his arm. "I believe you. I don't know how he thinks he can get away with this. All we have to do is get a statement from both of the paramedics."

"That will be easy to do, but it may not be enough in court. We need to find out where he cut her up. If we can find it, maybe we can at least get some of his fingerprints there. It would be even better if we could prove he owns it."

First they contacted the paramedics. They gave a statement confirming Kevin said he killed Tamara. Then they discussed how to find his place of horror.

Roxy asked, "Have they impounded his car yet? Who knows, maybe we could find a clue there."

"I don't know. Let me check."

"If they have it and haven't searched it yet, we should be there when they do."

"Good idea." Lee made a phone call and found out the car had been impounded. "Have they started examining it yet?" He listened intently to the person on the other end of the line. "Okay, tell them not to start until Roxy and I get there."

He turned to Roxy, "The car's been impounded. We gotta go! They're ready to start searching it. They'll hold off 'til we get there."

They raced to the impound lot. The search team stood by, waiting for Lee and Roxy to put on gloves.

They thoroughly searched the exterior of the car. No blood or anything else indicating something sinister happened on the outside.

When they opened the trunk, the first thing they noticed was a chainsaw. It looked like Kevin had wiped it clean. However, tiny specs of what could be blood was observed in a few areas.

Roxy became hopeful.

Lee ordered the chainsaw to be checked thoroughly for blood.

Lee turned to Roxy. "Now if only we could find out where he cut up her body, we might have a solid case."

The words no sooner came out of his mouth than the police chief called Lee.

"Hi Chief, what's up?" said Lee.

"You and Roxy have been working on the murder of a woman who was cut into pieces, right?"

Suddenly Lee's attention picked up. "Yes, we have. Why do you ask?"

Because there's a possibility someone found where she was chopped up."

Lee, now all ears asked, "Where?"

"In some forest outside of Jamesburg. Since it could be connected to your case, I'm assigning it to you and Roxy. You need to get out there right now. I was told you need to bring something to keep blood from getting on your shoes."

"Okay Roxy and I will check it out." He immediately turned to Roxy. "Someone may have found where Tamara's killer cut up her body. It must be pretty gruesome since the chief told me we need something to protect our shoes from getting blood on them."

"Okay," Roxy replied. "I have something we can put over our shoes at my house."

Lee dropped her off and they made plans to meet within fifteen minutes at an intersection near the location the Chief gave Lee.

Roxy parked her car at a gas station close to where Skip and Alva met the police. They easily found the forest the Chief told Lee about since the cop car still had its lights flashing. One of the cops was waiting for them. He escorted them to the site of the bloodshed.

"Good God!" Lee remarked. "It certainly looks like someone could have been cut up here."

Roxy gave him what she brought to cover their shoes with. Then they stepped into the horrifying mess someone left behind.

Lee asked one of the cops, "What makes you think this might be a murder scene?"

The officer who found the necklace held it up for Lee and Roxy to see.

"I guess that's enough to suspect a homicide," Roxy retorted. "Have you found anything else that could indicate if a body was cut up here?"

"No, nothing." The other cop said.

Lee took in a deep breath and told the cops, "Okay, stop looking. I'll get CSI out here." He made a call and not long afterward, crime scene investigators arrived.

When they started their investigation, Lee showed one of them the necklace. "Can you quickly do what you need to do with this so I can take it somewhere? I think I know how to find out who the victim was."

The necklace was tagged and placed in a sealed plastic bag. Then Lee and Roxy left the scene with the necklace.

Roxy picked up her car from the gas station. She took her car home and Lee picked her up there. Then they both went to the apartment Tamara's mother lived in. She was very visibly upset.

"Have you found out where Tamara is?"

Roxy took the plastic bag out of her pocket. "Mrs. Garrett, we need to show you something. Have you ever seen this necklace?" She showed the necklace to the distraught woman. Tamara's mother reached for it as she broke out crying.

"It's Tamara's necklace. I bought it for her on her eighteenth birthday."

Roxy pulled back the plastic bag before she could take it from her. "I can't let you have it. It's evidence from a crime scene. You're sure it's hers?"

"Yes, it has a silver whale on it. She has always loved the Orca whales here in the Pacific Northwest. Where did you find it?"

The next thing Roxy had to do was something she always hated. It was the worst part of her job.

"I'm so sorry to tell you that it looks like your daughter has been murdered and part of her body has been found in a dumpster."

She barely finished saying it when Tamara's mother started weeping uncontrollably. Roxy handed the necklace to Lee and put her arms around the grieving woman to comfort her.

"Now if only any blood found on the chainsaw

proves to be Tamara's and matches blood from the forest, we will be able to prove Kevin is a vicious killer," Lee said as they left Mrs. Garrett's apartment.

Chapter 37

A few days later, Lee and Roxy visited Maggie.

Roxy related, "We arrested the man who killed and cut up the woman whose body parts you and Peachie found. At least you don't have to be afraid of discovering body parts in a dumpster anymore, Maggie."

"That's wonderful. Thank you for finding a place for me to live. Maggie hugged them both. I have something to tell you. They've brought Peachie here too. They are working on getting both of us a permanent place for good. Would you like to see Peachie?"

We'd love to see Peachie," Roxy replied.

"I'll go get her," Maggie said as she turned and started down a hallway.

A few minutes later, she returned with Peachie right behind her. Peachie ran up and hugged both of them. "I can't tell ya how thankful we are. We'll never forget ya. We're gonna git our own place soon. They're tryin ta git us a place together."

"If there is ever anything you need, call me," Lee said.

"Looks like I kin stop havin nightmares," Peachie said. "Bout findin bodies in dumpsters now."

After leaving Maggie, they needed to finish a lot of loose ends connected to the case. One thing they wanted to accomplish was to meet with the swingers and give them an update relating to Tamara's murder. They met in Victor and Angela's apartment.

Katrina had come to terms concerning Ron's death and his affair with Anita. Hazel was still mourning Manny's murder. Anita missed Ron and frequently thought about the plans they made together. Whenever Joseph came to mind, she understood he killed Ron because he loved her, but it didn't make it any easier.

Lee and Roxy didn't ask any of them about their sex lives, but it didn't mean they wouldn't have liked to inquire about it.

It looked like all of the remaining members of the swinger group now seemed to be getting along okay with each other. Old hatreds had been healed.

Lee looked at each of them, then said, "We wanted to let you all know we arrested the man who killed Tamara Garrett. His name is Kevin Forester."

"Oh," Victor said, "I think we all knew him from the parties the owner gave."

Hazel chimed in, "Yes, Tamara talked about him the last time I talked to her. She told me he was one of the affairs she was having at the time. Do you know why he killed her?"

"At first he denied killing her, but we proved he did," Roxy said. "He finally told us he killed her because she threatened to tell his wife about the affair if he didn't leave her."

"She must have finally fallen in love with one of the numerous men she had affairs with," Hazel sarcastically quipped. "Too bad it killed her."

Katrina remarked, "I just hope that's the end of the murders in this apartment complex."

Everyone else nodded and gave a positive response. With that, Lee and Roxy left the swinger group and hoped they would never have to meet them again for the same reason.

Chapter 38

Lee and Roxy assured the swingers that as far as they knew there should be no more murders. The only thing they wanted now was to live their lives without fear. Everyone wanted to get back to where their secret world had been in the past.

The next day Katrina called Victor. She had stopped mourning for her two-timing husband and was ready to move on. "I think we should have another pool party and invite the two new couples that are interested in joining our group. We need to do some celebrating."

"I agree. It sounds like a good idea. If you want to let everyone else know, I'll get everything ready. We can play Twister and Chicken Fight again."

He gave her the phone numbers of the couples who wanted to be part of the group. A few minutes later, she called him back saying the two new couples would definitely be there for the party.

Victor called the manager and asked him to close the pool for the party. He said he would and as soon as he put a sign up and locked the pool door, he brought Victor the key.

Making a trip to the store Victor bought the same finger food they had the last time. This time he also bought drinks since he and Angela didn't have enough for everyone. After Victor put the tables together, Angela brought down paper plates and cups. She also brought down the bath towels.

When everything was set up, Victor called Katrina. "Call everybody and let them know we're ready to party."

Katrina called the rest of the group plus the two new couples to let them know everything was ready. It didn't take long for the group members to arrive. A few minutes later the two new couples arrived. Victor closed and locked the door.

Everyone sat down at the tables. Angela and Victor already knew the two new couples. They met at another gathering of swingers in a nearby community. They had been surprised to find out they also lived in Jamesburg.

Victor introduced them to the group. Placing his hand on the shoulder of the man sitting next to him he said, "This is Buddy Durham and his wife Bertha." The other three women left in the group greeted them with enthusiasm. Then he motioned to the other couple sitting across from him. "This is Maxwell Lindale and his wife Kendra." They were also welcomed to the group.

Victor threw up his hands and said, "Okay, let's eat."

"This food looks great," Maxwell remarked.

"I agree," said Buddy.

"You're going to find," Katrina stated, "that Victor always does a wonderful job whenever we have a party."

They dug into the food with substantial appetites, all eating enthusiastically and enjoying every bite. While they ate, the murders of Ron, Manny, Christopher and Tamara came up. The two new couples had already heard of the murders, but wanted to know a little more about them.

Buddy was the first to ask about the killings. "Why was Ron killed?"

"I'll take that one Katrina said, "He was having an affair with Anita."

Buddy looked at Anita and asked, "With you?"

"Yes, Katrina is right. I was having an affair with *her* cheating husband."

Katrina nodded. "However, I have forgiven Anita, but not my husband."

"And Joseph also killed Manny because he found out he killed Ron." Hazel said.

"I can't believe one of the detectives killed Christopher Lockhart, "Kendra commented.

"Yeah, he threatened us," Hazel said. "So she decided to kill him because she had been a swinger herself."

Maxwell said, "Is it true that Ron, Christopher and Tamara's bodies were cut up and discarded in dumpsters?"

Angela shivered and replied, "Yes, It's true. It's disgusting just to think of it."

Bertha said, "I've heard Tamara wasn't a swinger. So why was *she* killed?" she asked.

Victor answered, "She threatened to tell his wife about their affair."

Buddy let out a low whistle. "Wow, that's a lot of shit that went on here. I'll bet you guys are glad it's over."

Katrina nodded. "Yeah, we sure are. Maybe we shouldn't jinx it by talking about it."

Everyone agreed. When they finished eating, Victor stood and said, "We had so much fun playing a couple of games at our last party, we're going to play them again."

Maxwell clapped his hands. "We're always up to playing games. Bring 'em on."

Victor laid out the plastic mat for the game. He took their four guests aside to explain the game to them. "I'm going to spin this dial and you each have to take off a piece of clothing and put your hand or foot on one of the colored circles. It gets real interesting as the game goes on because you are allowed to fondle or kiss whoever you want."

Buddy exclaimed, "Wow! I love this game already."

During the game, Maxwell fondled Katrina's breasts and kissed Hazel. Buddy fondled Anita's breasts and kissed Angela. The ladies all fondled the men's genitals.

When the game ended, everyone was excited to start the next game.

Victor announced that they would be playing Chicken Fight in the pool.

Buddy declared, "We've all played this game before. So let's get going." He ran and jumped into the pool.

The rest of the group also jumped into the pool.

Katrina hopped onto Buddy's back. Anita sprung onto Maxwell's shoulders and Bertha climbed onto Victor's back. Kendra jumped onto Hazel's shoulders while Angela waited for one of the aggressors to be toppled. The first one to be thrown off someone's back was Anita. Angela climbed onto Maxwell's back and started pushing Katrina off Buddy's shoulders. A great deal of screams, oophs and ohs ensued.

Everyone was tired out, but extremely cheerful by the time the game ended. They anxiously awaited the next facet of the evening.

"Time to head up to our apartment," said Victor. "Angela's got the front room ready for an orgy."

It didn't take long for the swingers to exit the pool. They didn't even dress. Grabbing towels, they wrapped themselves and ran down the hall toward the lover's den.

Chapter 39

About a week later, Lee and Roxy sat in a restaurant relaxing over lunch. The case had been a long and puzzling one, with a twist at every turn. They discussed the strange aspects of the case as they ate.

"I can't believe how many killings there were," Roxy said . "Three men and one woman."

"What was really strange is they were all killed for different reasons," Lee replied.

"Plus three of the bodies were cut up and dropped into dumpsters." Roxy said as she frowned. "Ugh! How disgusting that was."

Lee held his hand up. "And we had all those swingers involved too."

Emotion showed on Roxy's face. "I'm so sorry about Cat. I still don't understand why she would kill someone no matter what they did unless it was in the line of duty."

"I don't know either. I never will understand why. I guess the fact that she had been a swinger must have consumed her. Maybe she thought that would take away her feelings of guilt."

They hadn't finished eating when Lee's phone rang. He ended the call and turned to Roxy. "Take a big gulp of what you've got on your plate. We're being called to a new case. It's a really weird murder. Something I've never heard of before. I'll tell you about it in the car."

About the Author

Amber LaCorte spent her childhood in Michigan, but has lived in several other states, including Arizona, Nevada and Kentucky. She has resided in western Washington for over forty years. Her reading interests have always been murder mysteries. It's no surprise that the books she writes are of the same genre.

Acknowledgements

I want to thank the following people. They have all been great inspirations for me:

My Son. He's the one who gave me the idea for this book.

The rest of my family who think family is an important part of our lives.

Charlie, who has given me the reason to want to succeed.

The friends who have given me the encouragement to keep writing: Bonnie, Rebecca, Barb and Jan.

My editor, Larry Krackle, who kept me on track and kept telling me I could do it.

Everyone in my writer's group who always give me great critiques.

Last but not least the following people who have been waiting for my book to be finished: Lee, Steve, Vic, Louie, both Rons, Ed, Virginia, Tony and Mary.

Plus anyone else I may have inadvertantly forgotten.